THAT TIME OF YEAR

Other titles by Marie NDiaye
available from Two Lines Press

MY HEART HEMMED IN

SELF-PORTRAIT IN GREEN

ALL MY FRIENDS

THAT TIME OF YEAR

MARIE NDIAYE

TRANSLATED FROM FRENCH
BY JORDAN STUMP

TWO LINES
PRESS

Originally published as: *Un temps de saison*
© 1994 by Editions de Minuit
7 rue Bernard-Palissy, 75006 Paris
Translation © 2020 by Jordan Stump
All rights reserved.

Two Lines Press
582 Market Street, Suite 700, San Francisco, CA 94104
www.twolinespress.com

ISBN: 978-1-931883-91-7
Ebook ISBN: 978-1-931883-92-4

Cover design by Gabriele Wilson
Design by Sloane | Samuel
Cover image from FELT, a dance production by Elisabeth
Schilling, with design by Mélanie Planchard. Photograph by
Martine Pinnel.
Printed in Canada

Library of Congress Cataloging-in-Publication Data:
Names: NDiaye, Marie, author. | Stump, Jordan, 1959– translator.
Title: That time of year / Marie NDiaye; translated by Jordan Stump.
Other titles: Un temps de saison. English
Description: San Francisco, CA: Two Lines Press, [2020]
Identifiers: LCCN 2019052039 (print) | LCCN 2019052040 (ebook)
ISBN 9781931883917 (hardcover) | ISBN 9781931883924 (ebook)
Subjects: LCSH: Psychological fiction.
Classification: LCC PQ2674.D53 T4613 2020 (print)
LCC PQ2674.D53 (ebook) | DDC 843/.914--dc23
LC record available at https://lccn.loc.gov/2019052039
LC ebook record available at https://lccn.loc.gov/2019052040

1 3 5 7 9 10 8 6 4 2

This work received support from the French Ministry of Foreign
Affairs and the Cultural Services of the French Embassy in the
United States through their publishing assistance program. This
project is also supported in part by an award from
the National Endowment for the Arts.

PART ONE

1 – Night had fallen by the time the teacher made up his mind to go out in search of news. The lights of the nearby farm were half blotted out by the fog, and beneath his anxiety the teacher was happy to think he'd be leaving the next day, because once August was over life here was clearly lived amid unending rain and mist, as he hadn't known before, as this afternoon had abruptly taught him. "Just imagine living here year-round! Not for me, no thank you!" he muttered in disgust as he started down the path to the farm, testing the terrain ahead with the tip of his shoe before every step, so dim was the light of the moon.

The cold seemed to have come on all at once, just after lunch, as the teacher and his wife were tranquilly talking over their plans to return to the capital the next day, the second of September, a little later than usual. Suddenly a shiver ran through them both, and the teacher offered a few wise thoughts on the changing seasons. Had they perhaps delighted a little too smugly in their approaching departure, their only regret being that the fair weather hadn't stayed with them for just one day more? It was certainly true that they'd never given a moment's thought to the climate or anything else of this place, once the thirty-first of August came and they headed homeward; their long, invariably happy, sunlit vacation at an end.

And now a misty rain was falling, and the teacher had no coat to put on.

Feeling the cold, he walked through the farmyard to the house, knocked on the door. No answer came, and he guessed someone was looking out a second-floor window to see who was there, perhaps having difficulty making out his face, possibly waiting to be sure they recognized him before coming down. Self-conscious, he took a step back, looked up. His forehead stung from the cold. "Just yesterday it was so nice," he blankly said to himself over and over, dismayed, suddenly despondent.

Finally the farmwoman opened the door a crack.

"I'm Herman," he called out, "the teacher, your neighbor."

"Oh yes, yes."

She opened the door wide, cordial and smiling but evidently not about to ask him in. She was a sturdy young woman with very red cheeks.

"Have you seen my wife and our son?" he asked.

He explained that Rose and the child had headed for the farm three hours before to buy eggs, so he was thinking they hadn't come back because Rose had lingered to chat, or maybe the child had insisted on saying goodbye to the animals. But now it was time they were home, and he himself, Herman, the teacher, had been worrying all this time, concurrently a little indignant, that Rose hadn't bothered to set his mind to rest with a phone call. His exasperation grew as he spoke.

"I'd like you to tell them I'm here," he said sharply.

He took a step forward, inserting his shoe between the woman's firmly planted feet, trying to protect at least his head from the spitting rain, but he immediately pulled it back, and even, blushing, began to retreat, because far from grasping that he wanted to come in and politely standing aside to make way, she stood rooted to the spot, still as affable as ever with her face slightly tilted toward him, the better to hear. A blouse printed with apple blossoms—worn by all married women in this region, he happened to know—encased her breasts, slightly compressing them, tied on one side by two laces of contrasting colors, which, if you were up on the local customs, told you what year she'd taken a husband. The scarlet of her cheeks was perfectly mirrored in the heart of each flower.

"Can't she see I'm soaking wet?" Herman asked himself, both shocked and submerged in a sort of numbness that erased all trace of anger.

Seeing her offer no answer, make no move, even as she went on staring at him with a strangely obliging gaze, he asked her again to bring him Rose and the boy, carefully enunciating each word. Longing for the next day, the day that would see all three of them back in the capital, he wearily told himself: "Oh, I'll never understand these people!"

She looked at him in surprise, and a little sound escaped her throat. She vaguely raised her arms in a sign of impotence—very pink, plump arms, bulging above the elbows where they emerged from the grip of the blouse's short sleeves.

"No one ever came here," she finally said. "We've seen no one today but the rural patrol."

"That's impossible!" cried Herman.

His exasperation came flooding back, spurred on by a terror he'd never felt before. He shook his index finger under the farmwoman's nose.

"First you claim no one came here today, and then suddenly you tell me the patrolman stopped by: it doesn't add up! In that case, why shouldn't you have seen my wife and son too, since they told me they were coming here to buy eggs?"

She was still smiling, surprised, silent. The teacher

sensed she'd stopped listening but was determined to go on displaying unshakable goodwill, perhaps out of respect for the time-honored duty to treat visitors courteously, overlook any offense, an obligation people around here traditionally honored, despite what they might be feeling inside. His worry was getting the better of him, he wasn't thinking straight. Rather than rushing right off to try to find where Rose and the boy might have gone, Herman was fixated on getting inside, shoving the woman out of the way if need be, then sitting down for a few moments, he thought, in the kitchen by the stove, where he could dry his clothes and try to calmly question this woman, who would have no choice but to concede that it was impossible she hadn't seen Rose and the child that afternoon if Herman could only show her, point by point, as he did with thick-headed students, that her first assertion didn't stand up to scrutiny.

"Let me explain," he insisted, with an edge in his voice. "I assure you, Rose came here. Where else would she have gone in this weather?"

"Not a warm day," the woman agreed.

And she went right on smiling. Whenever he spoke she delicately tilted her forehead his way, with an exquisite courtliness that rattled the teacher. Try as he might to maintain his poise, wasn't he showing a deeply deplorable disrespect, and wouldn't the villagers construct their sense of him based on what this woman would surely soon tell them of this encounter? For ten years he and Rose had been spending their summer vacations in this remote area, and he'd made it a point of pride to behave with the slightly superior civility he thought the only suitable stance for citizens of the capital, always intent on revealing their sophistication but too fine to make a show of it. And now, despite his best intentions, drunk with worry, he must seem like a boor in the eyes of this woman and everyone else around here, all these people with their oddly refined manners.

"Forgive me," he said, "it's just that, you understand, I can't think where my wife…"

"Yes of course, the weather changes so fast around here, you have to know it's coming."

Understanding that he was about to say goodbye, she widened her smile, gave him a bow, even stepped far enough outside to be dampened herself, elegantly pointing the way to the front gate—though there was no need, since Herman had come through it on his way into the courtyard—but with that gesture pushing helpful neighborliness to its furthest extreme. He returned her bow, feeling his awkwardness, and the rain fell on the back of his neck, slid down his spine. Shivering, he turned on his heels and slogged back toward the gate. The woman closed the door behind him, and immediately the house's ground floor was dark, which he couldn't help thinking slightly rude. He must have offended her enough that she believed she could justifiably limit the geniality of her face and gestures to when he was looking at her; for that matter, maybe the code governing behavior with outsiders, however rigorously welcoming it obliged one to be in their presence, did not stipulate that one had to go on helping once their backs were turned.

Herman set off running down the road. His panic returning, he saw from afar that no light was shining in his house, which meant Rose hadn't come home, so he immediately turned toward the village, still running, breathing heavily, throwing out little cries and involuntary interjections.

"Really, in weather like this," he hiccuped, frantic, "isn't it strange…it's scary… And the boy, out in the cold…"

And that abrupt drop in temperature put the finishing touch on his terror, convincing him that by waiting one day too long to go home and thus breaking with a ten-year habit, by letting September come to them here when September was a month they knew only in Paris, he and Rose had laid themselves open to unknown tribulations they might not be strong enough to withstand. Because what did they know of the fall around here, what did they know of these people's ways once all the outsiders were supposed to have left? The fact was that outside of summertime they knew nothing about the place at all.

"We have no idea what dangers we might face around here," Herman told himself, panting, "the rain, the wind on the back roads, these simple people who might not take kindly to strangers on their turf once the thirty-first of August has passed… How stupid, how blind…"

He didn't think for a moment that Rose might be in one of the many village shops: it would be unlike his wife to spend hours poring over merchandise. Nor did Rose and Herman or even the little boy have any friends they might be visiting in the village, they knew no one Herman could call on and ask if they might have seen Rose come by, although every day in the summertime they came down together to do their shopping, and everyone knew them by sight. But Herman strongly sensed that he mustn't let himself go running to anyone desperately asking after Rose. That would be a sort of indecently misplaced thing to do, even a grave transgression of the rules of deportment, whose specifics he nonetheless knew nothing about, even if he was beginning to grasp their spirit.

He slowed to a walk a little before the village's first houses, trying to force a casual gait in spite of his trembling legs, his dripping face.

"They're going to wonder why I don't have an umbrella," he told himself uneasily.

He walked three times around the deserted village square, hands in his pockets, and his shoulders were suddenly racked by outright convulsions. He hurried down the main street, heading for the gendarmerie.

However certain he was that he wouldn't see Rose inside, he couldn't help glancing into every shop he passed by, and he sensed that the owners, idle at this late hour, were also watching him as he passed, their expressions inexplicably disapproving. Was it, Herman wondered, because they were surprised to see him still here on the first of September, in the rain, in soaked shirt sleeves, finding that suspicious in itself? Maybe the people around here didn't like outsiders experiencing autumn, which was in a sense none of those outsiders' business, maybe they thought the intrusion into their mysterious post-summer life indiscreet? For a moment Herman was excited—his worry forgotten—to find himself here in the village in this season unknown to his fellow Parisians, who by now were all back in their apartments, vaguely assuming, as Herman once did, that the region they'd just abandoned had gone into hibernation, awaiting their return the next summer, perhaps preserved in a perpetual green mildness.

"If they only knew," thought Herman with a flush of pride, "how it rains here all day long from the first of September, not to mention the cold, they'd never dream! I'm going to have a good surprise for them, I'll tell you that…"

For the first time he noticed that the women behind the counters of the bakery, the charcuterie, and the hair salon all wore the same blouse he'd seen on his farmwoman neighbor, with the same scarlet-hearted apple blossom print, and it compressed their breasts in just the same way, and was tied with those same multicolored cords of very specific signification, which, Herman thought, gave them that formal, slightly haughty air and that ramrod posture, only their necks seeming to move fluidly, extending their heads toward their interlocutors as the farmwoman had so graciously done to express her attentiveness. In the hard white light of the shops, the little flowers' red-glowing hearts strew bloody dots over the women's immobilized busts as they bent their foreheads nearer the windows to observe Herman with their stern, severe eyes. They smiled when Herman looked back, but only with their lips, an almost urbane smile, excessively revealing their teeth. They dipped their heads in a rudimentary bow, their eyes looked down and then away, the blood-red flecks on their blouses rippling with that discreet movement.

Abashed, Herman stopped looking through the shop windows. He ran until he reached the gendarmerie, at the far end of the main street, among the village's very last houses, where the rows of streetlights came to an end and the Paris-bound national highway started. The building was dark. He pushed open the door all the same, and light filled the office the moment he entered, blinding him. He squinted, then cried out in relief: "Oh, so there's somebody here!" And his apprehension found some respite at last.

A gendarme was sitting at the one desk in the room, shifting his pen back and forth from hand to hand. He'd turned on the lamp as soon as the door opened, but Herman saw nothing to suggest he was waking from a nap. His eyes were bright, calm, attentive. Herman immediately headed toward the big gas heater purring in the corner, turned his shivering back to it, and let out an "Oh…" of almost painful contentment. He thought he saw the gendarme's gaze drift again and again to his shoes, made of fine, orange-tinted leather, unsuitable for walking the back roads.

"I've come about a serious matter," he began.

"Tomorrow. The office is closed."

The gendarme wasn't smiling, but his face radiated a deep, gentle courtesy that again left Herman at a loss. He thought he could justifiably assume that expression signified an eagerness to be helpful at any cost; as if, in spite of his words, the gendarme were crying out: "I am here to serve!"

Encouraged, Herman pretended he hadn't heard the gendarme's answer. He explained in detail that Rose and their eight-year-old son had disappeared, that they were supposed to go home the next day, emphasizing—a little absurdly, even to him—that in previous years they'd never once delayed their return to Paris. He asked the gendarme to take down his description of Rose and the boy. And as he spoke his anxiety began to swell again, until, drained, he felt his voice crack, his stomach tighten.

"You must understand," he repeated, though he knew he'd said more than enough, "I've never seen the fall here before, this rain, this biting cold... We were always gone by now, and we had no idea what happens here afterward."

The gendarme listened, sitting still, making no move to take notes, bent slightly toward Herman, every detail of his face marked by tact and distinction. A long silence followed Herman's speech, and he stood wearily rubbing his hands behind his back near the blazing heater. At last the gendarme gently raised his eyebrows, as if he'd been waiting to make sure his guest was done before answering, so as not to risk breaking the thread of his reasoning. He was a very young man with pale hair, vaguely yellow, incomparable to anything in nature—typical, Herman reminded himself, of the region.

"No such thing has ever been known to happen here," he said in a melodious voice. "As far back as I can recall, never once has a villager disappeared."

"We're not from the village," Herman murmured. "We live in Paris from September to June. And our summer house is outside of town, maybe 800 meters away."

"Ah, interesting."

The young man nodded, and the corners of his mouth mechanically pulled back into a respectful, formal smile. All at once—from that smile and from the gendarme's nonchalance, his almost flirtatious preciousness—Herman understood that he had no intention, tonight at least, of working on his case, of even just writing down what Herman had told him, and that his light, mannered tone might have no other goal than to tell him so without undue harshness.

Seeing him so disinclined to take an interest, Herman began to doubt that things would be any different the next morning.

"He doesn't care if anything happens to Parisians," he thought, "and if it does, it's not his problem."

"Once summer's over, once the thirty-first of

August has passed, then you want nothing more to do with us, do you? If we insist on staying till fall we do so at our own risk, we're all on our own, and no authority is going to protect us. As far as you're concerned we have no legal existence, that's how it is, isn't it?"

Offended, the gendarme shook his head. He assured Herman that at any time of year outsiders would find aid and protection from the local constabulary, and no gendarme had the right—not even the mayor had the right, or the town council, or the prefect—to decide otherwise.

"But do you ever have outsiders here in the fall? Or any season but high summer?" asked Herman, a little annoyed, less amiable than he would have liked.

"In truth, never."

And the young man ingratiatingly added that Herman was the first Parisian he'd ever seen in the autumn rain and the stinging cold that inevitably settled in on the first of September, not to leave again until the middle of June. He didn't say if he thought it was a good thing that a vacationer had crossed over the border of summer for the first time, if as a villager he found that development auspicious or galling. Herman was desperately curious to know. He folded his arms and put on a casual air.

"Is it in any way risky for me to stay here? Am I

in any danger of arousing the antipathy of the locals?"

"No, no, of course not!"

The young man smiled more broadly, made placating gestures with both hands, assured Herman that everyone here would be glad for the opportunity to deploy their hospitality, which for many was nothing short of a mania.

"And in any case, as soon as you find your family you'll go home, right?" he concluded, his tone slightly pleading, as if, thought Herman, the tightly clenched reins of perfect, codified politesse for a moment slipped slightly from his grasp.

"How will I ever find them without your help? You haven't even written down their descriptions!" Herman cried.

"Come back tomorrow. As I told you, this isn't the time. My shift officially ended an hour ago. I did turn off the light, and people generally don't come walking into a dark building."

Having said that, the gendarme gave a little bow, his eyes fixed on Herman's shoes. Herman sighed, then turned toward the heater to warm his belly a little. He couldn't bring himself to walk out into the rain, to go home—more than a kilometer away now—to end up adrift in the silent house, which he didn't know in such weather, and fret all through the night. But his clothes were now thoroughly dry, and he had no excuse to linger in the gendarmerie. He nodded to the young man and went out.

"My God, what do I do?" he moaned when he was outside.

Had he ever known such helplessness? He felt terribly weak, desperately ill-equipped to face a situation of this sort. Not wanting to pass the shops again, he decided to take the lane, a narrow road that bypassed the village and climbed directly to the plateau where his summer house stood, his and many others, all of them now closed up for the year. The rain was still coming down; the cold was sharper now that night had fallen. Herman pushed on as best he could through the dark, whimpering, "My God, my God" over and over in a shivering voice, and for the first time he thought it would have been a fine thing, that evening, to have a house in the village, nestled among all the others, to walk home on a brightly lit street where he might meet some acquaintance he could pour out his troubles to. Very likely under the influence of the gendarme's words, he found himself thinking that Rose and the child could never have disappeared if they had had such a house, if they'd simply emerged from one of these houses so huddled together that everyone must know everything that goes on in the houses next door, and if, rather than going off for eggs by the desolate country road that led to the farm—a road hemmed in by fields edged with tall mulberry hedges—they'd simply made for the nearby village grocery, which sold eggs from that very farm. No villager had ever disappeared, the gendarme claimed, and Herman wholeheartedly believed it. He was just as convinced that no such misadventure had ever befallen an outsider in the heart of the summer either, and since he and Rose were evidently the first to cross over into fall, they were the first to face the consequences of an untested experience.

"If there's going to be trouble, best to face it head on," Herman mumbled, trembling and terrified. "But will we be able to leave tomorrow? Oh, my God, my God…"

The start of the school year was five days away. He didn't want to question whether they would be in Paris before then, but already he was fearing the disorder set off in his very tidy mind by this encounter with autumn in the village; in the region which, as he stumbled hunched and cold along the lane, he no longer considered it a privilege to be.

"Cursed fall," he muttered, "cursed place! Another two weeks here and I'd be done for. But I won't have it said that we backed away from trouble, not even the little one."

He had some difficulty finding the house in the fog, unlit as it was by the garden lamps that shone

from dusk to dawn all summer on the adjoining lots.
The rooms were freezing cold and the house had no
heater. For ten years they'd been coming to this place,
and until the thirty-first of August Herman and Rose
had known nothing but unending warmth. Only
the sight of the pastures, dazzlingly green, almost
artificial-looking, made them suspect that it wasn't
the same all year round, but they never thought to ask
anyone to confirm that lazy assumption.

Herman lit the stove's four burners, pulled a
mattress into the kitchen. The cold and the primitive
conditions made his despair complete. The best thing
he could do, he thought, was try to get some sleep
so he could get up early in the morning and launch
a serious search. Remorsefully he told himself: "No
one could possibly be more feeble than me. Out there
on the lane my teeth were chattering in terror, and it
was for myself that I was trembling, not for my loved
ones. I'd never find the strength tonight to go scour
the road and the hedgerows. No: first thing tomorrow, I'll get the gendarmes to help me."

2 – But the next morning, recalling the previous evening's discussion with the very unhelpful gendarme,
he decided it would be smarter to talk to the mayor.

He knew the mayor had no direct power over the gendarmerie, but he vaguely reflected that the mayor was a sort of boss all the same, and in both age and education closer to him, Herman, than those young rural gendarmes, so surely he would quickly grasp the urgency of the matter, and would exert his moral influence to force an immediate inquest.

The clouds were low, the rain was still falling. Herman took his umbrella, but he had nothing to put on his feet except the flimsy pair of shoes that had drawn the gendarme's gaze, and they were still thoroughly soaked. For that matter, the ambient wetness seemed to have already impregnated his clothes, the mattress, even the furniture, which looked oddly dark and damp. His hair felt faintly wet, the house funereal.

"Everything's turned hostile all of a sudden," he groaned. "Is it because I've seen the fall, is this the price you have to pay?"

He slammed the door as he walked out, not locking it. And with that he made a wish not to cross the threshold of that house again until the next summer, whatever happened, and he even thought he'd been very reckless to come back without first ascertaining the dangers of acting on his own—flouting the laws and customs that must govern post-summer life in this place.

The front yard was already dotted with puddles the size of small ponds. He hopped over them gracelessly. His bones, he thought, his entrails, everything in him was similarly saturated, stiff and cold. He followed the lane down into town, now indifferent to the mud that splashed under his feet and soiled his pant legs. He went straight to the town hall and found it open, though it was only a little past eight. It was an old half-timber house, away from the center of town, across from the gendarmerie. From the street it was narrow and tall, but as soon as he stepped into the lobby, where he'd never been, Herman saw a long succession of rooms extending toward the back. A great many women in clacking high heels came and went from room to room, carrying files or thick binders, pens tucked behind their ears or thrust into their hair. He was taken aback by the extreme modernity of the furnishings and décor, remembering the city hall of his arrondissement back in the capital, its cramped little rooms, grimy wooden floors, yellowing walls, a scattering of cheap chairs. He was also surprised to see so many women at work here. They all wore the same outfit: a dark blue suit over that traditional blouse, whose colored ribbons hung from under the short jacket and bounced merrily on their hips. As for the rooms they were streaming out of, at the back of the building, Herman peered through the open doors but couldn't see to the end, and he concluded the rooms must have been six or seven deep.

Suddenly intimidated, ashamed of his filthy shoes, he approached a receptionist sitting up very straight behind a long glass desk.

"I'd like to see the mayor, it's serious."

"Do you have an appointment?" she asked in a metallic voice.

"No, no, but it's urgent, it's very urgent."

She raised her eyebrows, regretful, elegant, and undertook to explain that the affairs attended to by the mayor each day starting at seven in the morning were all, every one, of the greatest urgency, the rest were handed off to secretaries or functionaries, and she couldn't possibly let Herman take the place of someone who, for similarly urgent reasons, had requested an appointment sometimes weeks in advance.

"But my case is particularly serious!" Herman cried, though in truth he was already beaten.

Had he ever rebelled against administrative rules when they were rationally, implacably laid out for him? The receptionist demurely asked to be allowed to point out that every urgent case possessed the same exceptional seriousness in the eyes of the petitioner.

"Yes," said Herman, "but…"

"Would you like me to submit your case to a secretary?"

He jumped back in horror and sharply refused. Then, hoping to erase the memory of that reaction, he assumed a humble voice and asked what all these people were employed to do.

"It's a big township," the receptionist answered, a little surprised. "This is the seat of the canton, there are a great many problems and questions to see to."

He was still intrigued and unsatisfied. But, vaguely fearing that if he displayed his ignorance of the workings of the village's institutions he might be looked on less benevolently, he gravely nodded his head, doing his best to look as if he understood.

"Who's the most important auxiliary or aid, I mean the one closest to the mayor, whom I could see immediately?"

"Well, there's the president of the Chamber of Commerce," said the receptionist, with an attentive, engaging smile.

"She wants to help me," thought Herman.

He agreed at once, stammering out a few quick words of thanks. But his thoughts were darkened by deep discouragement, his will dissolving at the thought of wasting time with someone whose position gave Herman no reason to believe he might be of use in the search for Rose and the child. The receptionist stood up and asked him to follow her.

"These people are so considerate, so obliging," Herman told himself. "They're holding me captive, more securely than they ever could with orders and interdictions."

He then chided himself for having refused to have his case placed in the hands of a secretary, who might immediately have grasped its importance, even all its potential tragedy, and passed it straight on to the mayor. Because now, convinced Herman would be all the happier and more confident for it, the receptionist was informing him that the president of the Chamber of Commerce was also the head of the festivities committee. Herman was almost offended.

"That's not what I need at all," he said, a little too loudly.

And his eyes stung with helplessness. The receptionist pretended not to have heard him, out of tact, he supposed. She led him to a steep, narrow stairway that spiraled up from the lobby. As she walked in front of him, he noticed her blouse had no ribbons: it must have been secured by a clip on that side.

"So she's not married," he told himself, proud of his penetrating eye.

They climbed to the fourth floor, the receptionist quick and lithe, Herman trudging. The woman's calves were oddly muscular and bulging, and

that—combined with the lack of ribbons and the so-
licitousness that in this place sometimes came close
to a languorous caress (the gendarme had taken that
same honeyed tone with Herman)—vaguely stirred
him. No one in Paris would have spoken to him so
caringly, and no one would have gone to such lengths
to make him feel they had no greater desire than to
serve him, even if all manner of obstacles Herman
couldn't quite make out had so far prevented any ac-
tual help from being given.

"I have to be careful not to complain, and not
to make any demands," Herman told himself in a
sudden surge of gratitude toward the receptionist.
"Everyone here knows their job, and for that matter
my case might already be known to more people than
I imagine; maybe at this very moment the mayor is
considering the steps to be taken even while someone is briefing him on one of those urgent matters
they sometimes have to wait so long to have attended
to…"

Assuaged, trusting, he wordlessly accompa-
nied the receptionist down a hallway that vanished
into the back of the building, very straight, so long
that Herman lost any clear sense of the village's
dimensions.

"How could this building be so deep?" he
whispered.

"Why, we're under the hill now!"

The receptionist stifled a little laugh, then gave him an almost tenderly reproachful glance over her shoulder.

"Don't you know? All the houses on the main street are built into the hill. It's very hard not to know that here."

"Forgive me," answered Herman, red-faced.

They walked past a tinted-glass door, through which Herman glimpsed a sizable conference room and many faces around a table, some of which he recognized: the village fishmonger was there; the grocer and her husband; a café owner; the *charcutière*, all poring over papers or, pen in hand, listening to someone Herman didn't have time to see. Intrigued to find all these merchants gathered on the fourth floor of the town hall—people he'd never pictured away from their shops, now divested of their aprons, almost enigmatic—his curiosity got the better of him, and he asked the receptionist what they were doing there.

"From what I could see, they were all shopkeepers," he added, lowering his voice, sensing he'd already shown a lack of discretion.

"Well, that's the weekly assembly."

This time she stopped and turned toward Herman, her pale, smooth face registering a surprise that worried him and immediately made him regret his inquisitiveness.

"Aren't you from the village?"

"No," he murmured. "Actually, I'm a Parisian."

She let out a polite, distant little "Oh!" then whirled around and walked on without a word. But her back and hips were stiffer now, her gait quicker and more businesslike, thought Herman, and he felt more distressed than he would have imagined, saddened and afraid in a way he thought excessive.

"Anyway, what harm can this receptionist possibly do me? She doesn't even know what I'm here for."

He gave a little laugh, trying to put on a good front. Reaching the end of the hallway, the young woman knocked on a door, opened it, then stepped aside to let Herman through.

"Here we are. I'll be on my way."

She strode off before he could thank her as he was planning, to his deep mortification. The president of the Chamber of Commerce—a short, wide man with a big drooping mustache—came forward, hand outstretched and pointing at the receptionist, still in sight, very small now, down the endless hallway.

"Did you notice? She doesn't have any ribbons."

"Meaning what?" Herman asked coldly.

"Meaning you can talk to her in a certain way, and she'll answer the same way."

"That's barbaric!" cried Herman, furious and disgusted. "What archaic customs! I can talk however I please to whomever I please."

"But it's very exciting this way," the president said in surprise.

"I'm not from around here," Herman interrupted.

Trembling with anger, he stepped into the office and looked around at the posters hung on the wall, showing various views of the region. It was a windowless little room ("We're under the hill," he reminded himself), thick with the smell of damp and saltpeter. Indignant at the manner of the president whose appearance alone, pudgy and unctuous, seemed to lessen the chances of his case being solved, Herman crossed his arms and raised his chin, determined not to speak first. Were it not for the prospect of a long walk back, he would have left then and there.

"Where are you from, then?" asked the president, jovial, manifestly delighted at Herman's visit. "From C.? From M.?"

He had named two nearby villages.

"I live in Paris. I should have been home yesterday."

The man let out a cry of astonishment.

"You're a Parisian? But summer's over!"

"That's what I'm saying," answered Herman, impatiently. "I'm only here because something terrible has happened."

And to himself, he said, "Although we did insist on waiting till the second to go home, God knows why, knowing perfectly well we were crossing the line into fall, even if we had no sense of what fall means here."

"Well now, that's extraordinary," the president cried.

He was suddenly very animated, his face deep red, and he looked at Herman with an irritating stare of disbelief. Herman did his best to be distant and superior, but saying the words "something terrible" had brought all the misery of his situation crashing down on him again. And so, he thought, rather than expressing his dislike for his host, he would do better to give him a quick summary of his misfortune, then go off and start his own search. He pulled up a chair, sat down on the edge, took his head in his hands, and in a dull voice recounted Rose and the boy's disappearance and how he was shown to this office instead of the mayor's after his failure at the gendarmerie the evening before.

"Oh, I can just see all that," the president said slowly and emphatically, now ensconced behind his desk.

"There's probably not much you can do for me."

"More than you think, much more."

Dully, Herman observed that every picture of the

region had been taken during the summertime. It was all cows and pastures, gentle wooded hillsides, skies unmarred by the slightest stippling of cloud.

Still as enthusiastic as ever, overflowing with a slightly abstract interest in Herman, the president went on:

"First of all, I'm going to see to it that the mayor hears of your misfortune, I mean before your turn comes to meet with him officially—not as easy as it seems, believe me, but at any rate I'll do what I can. That said, it's simply a formality, it will comfort you, nothing more. The mayor will listen gravely, give orders, make promises, but nothing will happen, and as a matter of fact there's nothing that can happen as things currently stand."

"But this is a very serious case, very urgent," Herman said, frustrated and out of patience.

"Oh, don't worry, he'll see that at once. Our mayor is a man of superior intelligence, a sort of sage, do you see? No, that's not the issue. Nor is the issue the power he does or does not have over the various authorities in the township. The fact is that our mayor can get essentially anything he wants—inquests, investigations, mobilizations of all the top men. He can get all the resources he asks for, but when it comes to results, that's another thing entirely, you understand."

"No I don't, I don't understand any of this, and it's not acceptable."

"The result depends on you, dear Monsieur, you must get that through your head."

At once grave and delighted, jubilant and serious, the president gave his desk a resounding smack. Herman vaguely sensed that some expertise this man had avidly acquired was finally finding an opportunity to come out, and that if Herman wished, it would take very little effort to gain this man's friendship. The mere thought of it disgusted him, but he was now ready to throw his lot in with anyone at all if it would serve his interests.

"What am I supposed to do, then?" he murmured.

"Well," said the president, his air wise and experienced, "the goal of our strategy, if I may put it that way, is to locate your family, or uncover information leading us to them. Very well. What do you do? Do you go out and question the townsfolk, plant yourself in front of them with your Parisian face and ask what they know? No! I know this place, people are as agreeable as can be but they only give outsiders the most superficial sort of help. You'll need great patience, a delicate touch, and you'll have to discreetly work your way into the life of the village, become a villager yourself—invisible, insignificant—and above all erase any memory of the fact that you're a Parisian who's stayed after summer, which is to say an intruder, who in theory has no right to see something that's none of his business, that never interested him before, that we'd rather he know nothing of: the long, springless winter existence that begins here with the month of September."

"But how long will that take?" asked Herman, dumbfounded.

"Oh, a long time, surely. You can't very well change your skin in two days, can you?"

"I haven't got that kind of time! The gendarmes..."

"I'm telling you, the gendarmes will only pretend to look. You're the one who will find your loved ones again, and for the moment no one here will want to help you, not even the mayor."

"What a horrible place this is!" cried Herman.

"No one will say it to your face, but they despise Parisians here."

The president leaned back almost proudly in his chair.

"I used to be one myself. And then, as it happened, purely by coincidence I stayed here till fall came, fifteen years ago it was, and I haven't left since. It all worked out beautifully, I became president of the Chamber of Commerce, head of the festivities committee, and now no one knows or remembers I belong to that hated race. I live in the Hôtel du

Relais, where I advise you to take a room at once, because obviously you're going to move out of your house on the plateau."

"I wasn't planning on setting foot in it again," said Herman loftily.

"Good. In fact I recommend you forget it entirely, forget everything that attaches you to the life you led here as a Parisian vacationer. Watch what you say. And you'll find that, little by little, without your even knowing it's happening, you'll be led to your wife and child, and then, who knows, then maybe you won't be too happy."

Herman shrugged, too outraged to answer. The president's unmistakable pleasure in taking on his case, the almost carnal delight illuminating his sly little eyes, left Herman dubious and wary. But he felt too weak, too alone, too helpless to spit out a scornful dismissal of the plan this man was urging on him. Besides, he had to admit, he had no particular grounds for thinking the president was trying to hoodwink him. On the contrary, it was a kind of humility, he thought, the humility of a man deeply committed to his cause, ready to make any number of personal sacrifices, that radiated from the president's ardent manner.

The president delightedly rubbed his hands. In his joy, he hurried on:

"As a former Parisian myself, and so, shall we say, a compatriot of yours, allow me to take possession of you just a little, to make of you, just a little, my work, my son! You mustn't hold anything back from me. I know everything there is to know about the village; in fact, I'd go so far as to say I've acquired a power here that can't be questioned. If you have a problem, listen to no one but me. Oh, speaking of power…"

He put on an anxious face and tapped one finger against his forehead. To his own disgust, Herman felt himself meekly slipping into acquiescence. After all, who was this man sitting before him? A nobody, an underling—once summer's over, he probably does nothing but head the festivities committee. And what festivities could anyone possibly organize in this endless rain? But at the same time, it wasn't unpleasant to have unburdened himself to someone. Suddenly Herman was so tired that he might not have gotten up from his chair, scarcely would have turned his head, if someone told him the mayor was walking by in the hallway. He listened with a distracted ear, as if his case had just been brought to a happy conclusion.

"I forgot to tell you about the merchants. They're the largest and most influential body in our village. Some say they've run the whole village for the past hundred years. They're holding their little weekly meeting today, right in this very building, on this very floor. You have to be a merchant to attend, and since they're smart and careful no one ever knows what gets said in there, everybody just assumes they're devising new ways to increase their power and profits. They've got a stranglehold on the mayor, almost all of them have a seat on the town council. They place their children in all the region's key positions, for instance the bakers' son is now secretary to the prefect, fifty kilometers from here, and the owners of the Relais have a son who plays tennis with the district councilor every week, not to mention that many of them have special connections, close or distant, with the heads of the gendarmerie or the fire brigade. For your own safety, I'll tell you straight out what I think: the merchants of this place are a bad lot, dangerous, cunning, their tentacles go everywhere; they're as rich as kings but plead poverty and sigh and wring their hands as soon as someone says the word 'money.' Be careful, but be smart: try to make friends with a few of them, but steer clear of their indecipherable, infinitely varied, ever-changing rivalries. I wouldn't be surprised if, without breathing a word of it to you, the merchants lead you to the very people you're looking for; I wouldn't be surprised to have it confirmed that they're up on all the deepest, darkest things that go on in the village. Who knows? Maybe they're talking about you at this very moment!"

The president erupted into a merry laugh. Herman shivered.

"All right, enough of this," he thought, but he didn't move, as if bound to his chair by weariness and an undefined fear of what awaited him outside.

But his host got up from his desk, came and stood before Herman, and clasped his hand between his own two hands, which were shaded by a dense mass of long hairs.

"I can't tell you how grateful I am for this opportunity," he said in a genuinely moved voice, "to take on a worthy project, serving as your guide and at the same time testing the observations I've made here the past fifteen years. Please don't let me down. Please, in a sense, be faithful to me. Be docile, learn from me, practice doing as I do. Nothing here is like what you know in Paris, people don't speak the same way, there are other laws, other customs. I don't miss it. Such a beautiful life I've made for myself here!"

Tightly encased in a pair of corduroy pants, the president's thighs twitched and jerked in what seemed a slightly overheated delight. Each thigh was as thick as both of Herman's, which were excessively slender and weedy under the linen of his summer suit. Herman was stifling in the airless little room, oppressed by the president's fervor. No one had ever given him such an effusive, heartfelt handshake, never had anyone but intimate acquaintances stood so close to him, knee to knee, and as a math teacher Herman never did anything to encourage such impulses.

"All right, let's get out of here," he told himself.

He disengaged his hand, finally stood up. His legs were trembling with fatigue. The president stepped back toward his desk, still smiling with confidence and affection, and Herman thought he'd noticed his exhaustion and was glad about it. He picked up the receiver of his desk phone.

"I'll have the Relais people send their little Charlotte to come get you," he said with a wink.

"What? Why is that?"

"Because you're going to take a room this morning, and then we'll see."

"I have other things to do at the moment," said Herman peevishly.

"No, you don't. What could you possibly have to do? I've told you, you won't get in to see the mayor, and there's no point to knocking at the gendarmes' door. It's very simple: you have to begin your life as a villager. And for that you need a room."

"I can get to the Relais on my own."

"It will look much better if you have Charlotte take you there," the president said categorically. "Knowing you've just come from my office, they won't ask any questions. Otherwise they'll wonder what you could be doing at the hotel in this season. Please, stop arguing, trust me. Not to mention"—he smiled knowingly—"that dear little Charlotte has no ribbons, nor even the prospect or the promise of ribbons to come."

"Again these archaic rituals!" Herman exclaimed, exaggerating his sneer.

"They're very good, they're exquisite. They keep me in a state of…of perpetual effervescence."

And the president laughed again, teasing Herman with gestures he didn't fully understand, with a friendly, indulgent mockery that Herman found repellent. No one had ever spoken to him with such cajoling condescension. Herman was used to giving commands and directions, and he tolerated no displays of intimacy, however decorous, especially in the absence of a longstanding friendship. He always spoke, and was always answered, with a certain coldness—neck stiff, back straight.

"And why should that change?" he asked himself.

He gave the president a vexed sidelong look. The president called the Relais and curtly ordered that they send Charlotte at once. Then he went back to telling Herman how he would have to behave from now on, as Herman slumped in his chair, drained of all emotion but unfocused hatred, perplexity, and regret, all centered on the president.

He was roused by the appearance of Charlotte. She half-heartedly held out her hand.

"Well, you took your time," said the president.

She shrugged. He delicately pinched her cheek and chuckled with feigned goodwill. Charlotte's pale pink face expressed only indifference. She'd hardly glanced at Herman as she said hello.

"Tell your mother to give my friend here room twelve, right next to mine," the president directed her. "Full meal plan, like me."

"And how much is this going to cost me?" thought Herman, roused from his torpor.

"All right then, see you this evening."

"So, ready?" asked Charlotte, seeing Herman still inert in his chair.

He jumped up to follow her down the hallway, still deserted and silent, and his weariness faded, his unease vanished as soon as the president's door closed behind them. He knew the way, but he didn't dare walk ahead of Charlotte, or even beside her. He sensed that for the moment at least he had to show absolute obedience to anyone willing to deal with him. But, remembering the president's words, he felt an irresistible need to defend himself.

"You know, I don't care what he says, I'm not his friend, not at all," he told her in a whisper, forcing himself to laugh.

They were passing by the merchants' meeting room. Herman stopped in his tracks.

"They're still there?"

"Of course they are, till noon," Charlotte answered in surprise. "Papa's leading the deliberations today."

"Oh, so your parents are members."

He was impressed in spite of himself. All at once he found the girl more interesting, and not only because the president had told him he'd find his way back to his loved ones by way of the merchants. In truth, he hadn't even remembered that promise at first.

"You don't want to be thought of as his friend," said Charlotte, "but he seems to want only good things for you."

Herman didn't answer. He ached to know what sort of things were being talked about on the other side of the wall, in the big conference room, and it was only with great difficulty that he held back from questioning Charlotte. She walked on with a leisurely gait, almost indolent, very different from the taut, resolute stride of the receptionist who'd led Herman down this hall in the other direction. He saw she was wearing the traditional blouse beneath her pink cardigan—no ribbons, just as the president had said—along with a pair of worn, dirty jeans and thick-soled tennis shoes. She wore her hair parted in the middle, and it hung limply down on either side of her face, its color the same whitish blond Herman thought he'd seen on every head in the village and the region. As for the equally blond president, Herman suspected his hair was dyed, though he had not pursued that conjecture with a more minute study.

"And what about me, if I'm supposed to become a real villager…" mused the brown-haired Herman.

He tried to laugh wryly, but a vague anxiety stopped him.

"Listen, tell me, what do they talk about in those meetings? You must know."

"Business. Who cares?"

"Are you proud that your parents are part of it?"

She shrugged, not turning around. Her voice was as sluggish and listless as her gait.

"This girl is just an idiot," he thought.

But the fact that on this of all days Charlotte's father was chairing the meeting, and that, additionally, the president had underscored her lack of ribbons or any hope of ribbons, however off-putting Herman had found that remark, those two pieces of information once again made him more sensitive than he would have imagined to the possibility of getting to know the girl, and perhaps learning more.

"Why doesn't she have a boyfriend, at her age,

with that nice face of hers? And what about that other woman, the receptionist? Oh, they'll be able to help me," thought Herman, "each in their way. I have to tell them about my problem first chance I get."

They made their way down the twisting staircase, ending up in the lobby just as the athletic-calved receptionist was striding by. She frowned and came over, without a glance Herman's way.

"What are you doing here, Charlotte? You know you have to ask me for a pass before you can go upstairs."

"I was in a hurry, they called me."

Charlotte made an impatient little gesture that ended in a limp wave, its cause all but forgotten. The receptionist sighed. A little surprised, Herman sensed that she was deeply agitated, her nostrils oddly flared.

"When you have time," she said, "stop by my place, okay?"

"Yes, yes, we'll see," said Charlotte with a quick, practiced smile.

She picked up her umbrella from where she'd left it by the front door and held it out to Herman, whereupon he remembered the distinctive trait of this region from the first of September to the end of May. The rain was pouring down, the main-street sidewalks were muddy, the light was so dim, even though it was nearly noon, that Herman would have found it hard to orient himself were it not for the glowing streetlights he found as he emerged from the town hall with Charlotte. When he asked, she told him the main street was lit day and night for the eight or nine months of the off season. Suddenly finding it all too much to bear, Herman wanted to run away. Like that morning, everything inside him seemed damp and mortified, shrunken, slowly rotting. He pulled his head down between his shoulders, bent forward, kept his eyes on his feet, and beside him Charlotte did the same, her fists in her jeans pockets. But the Relais wasn't far. Its wood and brick façade overlooked the main square. In previous years, coming down to the village and vaguely glancing at the Relais's windows, Herman had often told himself he would never spend a night in such a sad, dowdy hotel if he could help it. And now here was Charlotte ushering him into the little dining room and calling her mother, who soon appeared, slightly breathless, squeezed into her flowered blouse.

"This is a friend of Alfred's, we're supposed to put him in room 12," said Charlotte in her flat voice.

"Does he have a suitcase?" asked the mother. "Alfred's friends are always welcome."

And her little eyes narrowed with a simper whose meaning was lost on Herman. She abruptly held out a limp, warm hand.

"Not at the moment," said Herman, embarrassed.

She gave a little bow, humble, welcoming. She was wearing jeans like her daughter, and grimy-toed espadrilles.

"Full meal plan for him too."

"How much will this be?" asked Herman, making no attempt to hide his concern.

"A hundred and fifty for the room, two hundred for the three meals, plus twenty francs tax, which makes a grand total of three hundred and seventy."

The mother's tone was even warmer than before, courtly and deferential, and she stood bent slightly forward, her hands clasped over her belly, not looking Herman in the eye.

"That's far too much for me," he said briskly.

Annoyed, he let his gaze wander around the room and saw nothing that could justify such a price. Everything was plain and dull gray. Nonetheless, he resigned himself, since neither Charlotte nor her mother was answering him, and the mother was still frozen in mid-bow. Thinking he'd been rude, he blushed faintly. In any case, the president having decreed that Herman would take the full meal plan for the duration of his stay, Herman had to admit that at the moment he didn't have the courage, or a clear enough understanding of his situation, to make other arrangements. He sighed, then consented. The mother asked Charlotte to show him to his room, holding her bow until Herman was a few meters away.

"Charlotte doesn't make such a big production," he thought in relief.

More than anything, he was struck—unpleasantly—by those dirty espadrilles, so ill-matched to these elaborate displays of gentility.

3 – The room was tiny and looked onto the courtyard. Patting the wall, Charlotte confirmed that the president, Alfred, lived next door in room eleven, as if, Herman told himself, she were trying to reassure him, to certify that everything was just as he'd been promised. Then she went on her way, but he thought he heard her next door, in the president's room. She must have dropped onto the bed, which creaked and squeaked, informing him that sounds could clearly be heard from one room to the next, and even that they immediately identified their source. He thought he heard Charlotte mumbling, then humming. Her foot gently tapped the floor, keeping time. Herman listened blankly for a long moment, standing in the middle of the room, torn between the irritation of finding the lodgings so deficient and an amorphous,

tender pleasure he couldn't help feeling, knowing Charlotte was so nearby.

"Because she's going to help me," he mechanically repeated to himself. "The closer she is, the better for me. Given who she is, just think of all the things she must know!"

"Lunch is at one," Charlotte called to him, giving three little raps on her side of the wall.

Then she left, closing the door to room eleven, but, he noticed, not locking it. He went to the tiny window, dimmed by a thick grate. He managed to pull it open, and the rain came spraying in. What he saw below him hardly counted as a courtyard, more an uncovered storage area with a row of trashcans. But the room was on the top floor, and Herman had a view over the slate roofs studded with satellite dishes, to the hills beyond, now lost in the gloom. Directly facing him, the back side of the charcuterie only had one window as high as Herman's. He spotted a face, seemingly an old woman's face, watching him through the glass. Seeing him look back at her, she nodded several times in greeting, smiling insistently. Troubled, he closed the window, and through the bars he saw the woman still gazing toward his room.

He sat down on his bed and tried to consider his next move. Although he did his best to think of

Rose and the child with a compassion befitting their plight, his mind wandered, disoriented, and when it lingered on some thought it more often concerned the president or Charlotte or the receptionist than it did Rose and the boy, about whom he couldn't think of what to say to himself, except, with a little impatience, "How terrible!" He accused the abundantly flowered paper on the walls and ceiling of distracting him. Everything in this room irritated and repelled him: the chenille bedspread, the little armoire, the Formica table, the shag carpet. He wasn't used to this kind of world; he'd always lived in an atmosphere of refinement. Feeling oppressed, losing his spirit, and since the old woman was still spying on him, he got up to leave in spite of his fatigue, locking his door and going down to the dining room. It wasn't yet one o'clock, but the three big tables were already full. He had the disagreeable feeling that they'd been waiting for him, and when, from the end of the central table, the president approvingly waved him over and hailed him by his name, Herman hurried in, chiding himself even though he wasn't technically late. They'd saved him a place on the president's right, facing Charlotte. And the receptionist was there too, next to her.

"You eat lunch here?" Herman couldn't help but ask, surprised.

"Every day."

Smiling, she gestured toward the two other tables.

"Everyone who works at the town hall eats lunch at the Relais. Actually, we're required to."

"Even the mayor?"

"Oh no, not the mayor."

She laughed out loud, joined by all her colleagues who'd heard Herman's question.

"Why do you have to eat at the Relais?" he asked, hoping to put the moment behind him.

She paused and thought, slightly uncertain, then shrugged. All the others stayed silent, visibly not knowing how to answer. Suddenly sorry he'd asked, Herman sensed she was cross, not because she'd been exposed in her ignorance but because, for courtesy's sake, she felt forced to come up with an answer that would satisfy him.

"Maybe," she said, brightening, "maybe they want to be sure we're not late when work starts again at two." A murmur of agreement ran through the room. The colleagues, mostly women, kept their jackets on for lunch, the dark blue jackets Herman had seen them all wearing at the town hall, and some still had their pens in their hair, making them look as if they were still at work there in the dining room of the Relais, which Herman found slightly intimidating. The older woman beside him had some ten pens sticking out of her breast pocket, and two more in her hair. When Herman sat down, she pushed back her chair, leaned toward him, and wished him bon appétit. The president lay his hand on Herman's.

"So nice to see you again! We'll be side by side from now on, down here and upstairs. What do you think of your room?"

"There's someone looking at me through my window," Herman said quietly, pulling his hand away.

"Yes, that must be the charcutière's mother. Don't trouble yourself over her, she's perfectly fine. To tell you the truth, she sits at her window all day long, so…"

"But I don't like that, I don't like that at all, being watched," Herman whispered, put out.

"Well, that's how it is here, there's nothing you can do. When you're out, when you're home, someone's always watching you, what does it matter? Like I told you, you mustn't hide, quite the opposite, you have to let yourself be seen, you have to appear…absorbed, melded with the life of this place, just as I said. Be exemplary, show yourself, you have to lose every last bit of yourself, all right? Yes, let people see you, talk to you, invite you into their homes! You didn't lock the door to your room, did you?"

"Of course I did, why wouldn't I?"

"No, that's very bad!"

The president frowned, almost angry.

"Give me your key."

Herman reluctantly handed it over. The president passed it to Charlotte, whispered something in her ear, and Charlotte impassively left the table, dragging her feet slightly as always, just as her mother scuffed her espadrilles over the floor as she emerged from the kitchen with a big salad bowl of crudités, her upper body still bowed in the same affected, obsequious, but not entirely graceless pose Herman had seen two hours earlier.

"Charlotte's going to unlock your door," Alfred whispered. "Don't ever lock it again, people will wonder what you're hiding, and that would be the end of all your attempts to inspire confidence."

"Who's going to check to see if it's locked?"

"Oh, everyone, the other customers, our table-mates, all these ladies, maybe Métilde, everyone will find some pretext to go upstairs when you're out and have a look at your room, just to see."

The president broke into a spirited laugh, patting Herman's knee under the table. But Herman's dismay had waned the moment he heard the receptionist's name. Moved, he looked at her, and Métilde smiled back with an air of genuine friendship.

"Yes, you're going to help me," Herman said to himself, "and then…"

Flattered, happy, he was caught up in a sort of

euphoria that made him want to talk to everyone around him, to explain, to earn their pity and esteem. When Charlotte came back and sat down, he leaned toward her and Métilde, and in a voice loud and clear enough to be heard by everyone in the room he recounted at length what had happened to his family, his failure at the gendarmerie, the idea he'd first had of going to see the mayor. All the while, he studied the two women's faces respectfully turned toward his, their eyes attentive, their brows thoughtful. A flood of joy washed over him, and he forgot to be ashamed of it as he told them of Rose and his little boy. He didn't think anyone had ever listened to him so closely, so patiently, with such consideration and goodwill. Everyone around him had fallen silent. Frozen in mid-bow, Charlotte's mother pressed the salad bowl to her belly as if in prayer, meditative, drinking in Herman's words. The corners of Métilde's mouth were delicately turned up in a caring little smile. Herman exulted in feeling so tragic: Had anyone ever thought of him that way, had he ever, even once, moved someone? The thought of Rose turned abstract, supplanted by the intense pleasure of attracting the sympathy of the women around him, of holding their unknown, obscure minds in his grip.

When he finished, he glanced at the president. Alfred was contemplating him, leaning back in his chair. Herman couldn't make out if he approved. But he was vaguely troubled, once again, by the strange, unpleasant sense of a syrupy wave of affection pouring from Alfred's face, a face as fleshy and severe as a wary pasha's the moment Herman turned toward him, even briefly.

"Poor man," his neighbor with the many pens remarked in a soft, melodious voice.

She gave him a gracious smile, and, still sitting, made a kind of rudimentary curtsy, then went back to lunch, having put down her fork to hear Herman speak, like all the others. Then everyone stood up and came to press Herman's hand, murmuring a few formal words of sympathy. The women bowed down until their chignons grazed his forehead, the three or four male colleagues touched two joined fingers to their foreheads, faintly clicking their heels.

"Yes, poor man," said Métilde in her turn.

"Poor man," repeated Charlotte, in the same light, perfunctory tone.

All around the table, everyone was smiling at him with great benevolence and a forced but still charming display of sympathy. And Herman smiled back, disconcerted, seeing no way to get out of reciprocating this barrage of fine feelings. The meal went on, the discussion turned to professional matters. Herman's sad story never came up again. Métilde launched into

a quiet tête-à-tête with Charlotte, and Herman had
the impression she was chiding her for something;
Charlotte merely nodded in reply, agreeing with everything, imperturbably serene. Herman wished he'd
gone on a bit longer about his problem, asked these
people some questions, all these people who now
seemed so well disposed toward him, if they remembered what he'd just told them and understood the
gravity of the situation (which, from the look of it,
they didn't). No one was paying him any more mind
than they would a perfect stranger, who couldn't be
asked his opinion on the digitization of the survey
maps and to whom there was therefore nothing to say.

Defeated, Herman leaned toward the president.

"So what about my problem? Have they forgotten it already? No one had a single suggestion, nothing that could possibly help me."

"What makes you think your case is more important than any other?" Alfred whispered, shocked.
"I think you're making too much of it. Oh, it might
come up again, but really now, there are other things
to talk about, every bit as interesting: we've just ren-
ovated the town hall, everything's modern and new,
as you saw. Calm yourself, my dear friend, and be
patient."

He put his hand on Herman's knee and squeezed
it a little too hard. Irked, Herman stopped eating. A

deep sense of aloneness contracted his throat. He couldn't stop himself from asking Alfred:

"Well, where can they be? My wife, my son…"

"Oh, we'll see."

Alfred shrugged and tucked away a few healthy chunks of beef. But his indulgence toward Herman seemed bottomless. He often touched him, with his elbow, his foot, as if he didn't realize he was doing it, and soon Herman stopped noticing. He even asked if the president would like to finish the food on his plate, and Alfred eagerly accepted, fixing his gluttonous, tender, cunning eyes in turns on Herman and on the plate. As it happened, Alfred didn't care for that day's dessert. He stood up, clapped his hands, and declared it was time to get back to the office. Everyone immediately pushed back their chairs, desserts untouched. Diligently silent, they lined up behind Alfred in single file, took their raincoats and umbrellas from by the front door, and hurried out, hunching their shoulders. Only Charlotte stayed behind.

"That Alfred has a lot of authority," Herman observed.

"He's the office director," answered Charlotte, as if it were so obvious it didn't need to be said. She soon got up to help her mother clear the tables. Having nothing to do, Herman went back to his room; he was disappointed that he'd missed a chance to get closer to Charlotte, but the mother's presence, however discreet—and, in some way that still wasn't quite clear to Herman, pandering—bothered him. He had no doubt that the benevolently smiling mother had deliberately left them alone in a corner of the dining room. But Herman was determined to have a talk with her later concerning the price of his room and board, and he didn't want to have that talk after taking advantage of her faintly servile kindliness, which, he thought, she must reserve for guests she assumed were well-off. But the longing to talk to Charlotte tortured him, it even made his head spin a little. And he who had always loathed forwardness pictured himself taking Charlotte's arm, putting his face close to hers, giving her a gentle shake to convince her. He was sure she wouldn't be overly surprised. The sort of placid resignation he foresaw—already picturing it on her stolid face—gnawed at him painfully as he climbed the stairs, left him at once impatient and elated. It took some effort not to go straight back downstairs to take hold of Charlotte and bring to her face the submissive, unrepentant, unsurprised expression he found so mysterious.

"That girl is limp and dull," he told himself. "How could she possibly help me? But she must be twenty-seven or twenty-eight years old. Is she slow-witted? I'm not used to this sort of thing, I'm not used to it at all."

With her, he sensed, he had a boundless capacity for power and cruelty, which no one had ever let him glimpse before.

In his room he found a young man pacing back and forth from the bed to the armoire, who let out an infuriated little sigh when Herman came in. Suddenly tired, Herman fell onto the chair. He kept his back to the window, but through the rain he'd had time to see the watchful, smiling face of the old woman across the way, now so firmly pressed to the glass that her nose was misshapen. With a weary, distracted ear, he heard the young man eagerly introduce himself, standing before him, legs spread as if he feared Herman might try to flee. Who was he? Well, he was Gilbert, Charlotte's younger brother, the one who, as perhaps Herman already knew, played tennis every week with the district councilor, being the only inhabitant of the village—Gilbert that is—who knew how to hold a racket, that's why he and no one else had the good fortune to head off every Saturday to L., thirty kilometers away, where his tennis partner lived, for a friendly two-hour contest, summer and winter alike, for which—for that purpose alone, which must show Herman what kind of hope people here placed in his connections—his parents, the owners of

the Relais, had bought him a car, a bright-red little
205 turbo, so he could get to L. on his own after the
district councilor, Lemaître, his tennis partner, had
offered to come from L. every Saturday and pick him
up, so intent was he on having Gilbert for his weekly
tennis match. Did he, Herman, play tennis? When
he was a teenager, not since. And at the moment he
was literally exhausted; he was broken. Gilbert knew
Herman was a Parisian—which, to tell the truth, was
the real reason for his visit, so Herman could tell him
a little more about that, because Gilbert had every
reason to be extremely interested.

Vexed, Herman put a finger to his lips.

"Let's forget I'm a Parisian," he whispered. "For
the moment I'm not one, and I can't say when I'll ever
see Paris again."

"Oh, no, I'm not going to forget that!" Gilbert
cried.

And immediately his brow darkened, he looked
almost cruel. He was a tall young man with a handsome, hard face, as single-minded, determined, and
high-strung as Charlotte seemed tranquil and com-
placent. Although he grated on Herman's nerves,
the sort of blinkered resolve that clenched his jaw
amused and attracted him. So what did Gilbert want?
Nothing, besides making Herman's acquaintance,
now that they were neighbors. Because Gilbert lived

in room thirteen—he gently knocked on the wall over the head of the bed—just through there. At the same time he was very eager, once Herman could find the time to invite him in for a while (but, mused an anxious Herman, could he dare refuse to give a young man as manifestly impulsive as this all the time he might want?), to get Herman's advice and expertise on the possibilities that he, Gilbert, might have of finding a well-paid job in Paris, something in high-power business.

"Please, stop talking about Paris," said Herman softly, turning toward the window in spite of himself.

"Yes, yes, I know, your problem, your case!"

Gilbert gave a broad wave of disdain. Yes, he'd heard about it, what was the big deal? If something's meant to be found it turns up, if it's meant to be lost and forgotten no one will ever lay eyes on it again. So all Herman had to do was find out which of those his problem was, and then he'd understand, and there was no point in tormenting himself or trying to out-smart people.

Herman frowned and crossed his arms, but he was too tired to answer. Then Gilbert's face and man-ner abruptly changed. He smiled, put on a genial air and slightly flexed his knees, bending his upper body toward Herman, charmingly casual. A thick lock of fine, almost white hair slipped over his forehead. In a much gentler voice he told Herman he was going to organize a four-man tennis match, and Herman would be his partner against Lemaître and someone from L., no doubt a friend of Lemaître's—they'd have to see about that. It would be an interesting thing to do from many points of view.

Herman protested that he hadn't played in years. And the thought of a tennis match, however improbable the prospect, made him even more tired than before. There was nothing appealing about Gilbert—but how very flattering and captivating he could be... It was all because of this place's tradition of profound graciousness, because otherwise he was hardly even civil. He gave Herman the impression of a crude, menacing innocence, and he found it strangely agreeable not to resist him, although it wasn't long ago at all that he would have serenely scorned these naïve attempts to charm him or maybe wouldn't even have noticed them, wouldn't have seen them or felt them.

"I went to Paris once," said Gilbert, "but I didn't have the money to stick around."

He confided to Herman that he was counting on the district councilor, Lemaître, to give him a boost toward a comfortable, reasonably plush existence in Paris. Now he was counting on Herman too. Did Herman doubt the two of them could be friends?

With a smile, Gilbert assured him he knew just how to go about winning Herman over.

"Yes, we'll see," murmured Herman, on the point of falling asleep on his chair.

He thought he could feel Gilbert bending his pale, hairless face even closer, friendly, interested, aquiver with the little calculations and ruses churning in his mind, and now intent on Herman with a persistence that—Herman thought, half-dreaming—would soon surely turn tiresome. He had to try to get back to Paris before anyone asked him for help he didn't want to give, even as he was depending on everyone's help to solve his problem. So from here on out he would have to be careful not to cross anyone.

4 – He must have slept soundly for three or four hours, because he woke up in the dark. From his pitch-black room, he saw the window across the way blazing with light, but with no sign of the face. Even as he was feeling a rush of relief, the woman reappeared, as if she'd made out that Herman was up now. She smiled at him broadly, which gave her rumpled features a certain elegant beauty, then nodded, pleased to see Herman again, relaxed and open-hearted. Then she put her forehead to the windowpane and stayed

perfectly still. Slightly nettled, he wondered what had made her suspect he was awake and watching for her. What else could he conclude but that she'd felt it? He didn't dare close the curtain, out of consideration for her feelings. Not to mention that he feared any failure to observe the ways of the village, and the danger of her spreading it around that he'd just moved in and was already hiding.

He left the room; it was six o'clock. In the silent hotel, heading downstairs to the lobby, he couldn't shake the feeling that he was being spied on from every conceivable corner, but, he realized, he was growing used to the idea that he was never alone, no matter how it might seem, and even beginning to find, alongside his tenacious but fading resentment, a timid sort of pleasure in it.

Now he was outside, on the main street, his umbrella unfurled.

"How shameful," he told himself, "sleeping all afternoon instead of looking for Rose while it was light."

Then, almost gleefully, he hunched his shoulders, rounded his back, and set off for the town hall. This time he didn't glance into the shops, reflecting that he lived in the heart of the village now, and didn't have to face the inquisitive stares of the beribboned, breast-bound shopkeepers. Would they still look at him like that, seeing him come out of the Relais? Very possibly not, he told himself. So everything was going according to plan. He stopped to pick up a few things at the Co-op. He was almost out of money. And there was no bank or cash machine in the village. He'd have to go all the way to L., an undertaking whose prospect he found tedious and, though he didn't know why, worrisome. If not to be heading home to Paris, was it a good idea to leave the village?

In the town hall's vast, brightly lit lobby, he spotted Charlotte slumped on a chair, hands in her coat pockets, legs outstretched. Delighted at this excuse to go in, as he'd been wanting to do since he woke up not long before, he pushed open the glass door and cheerily hailed Charlotte, who answered him as always without surprise, pleasant and neutral. What was she doing here? She was waiting for Métilde, who got off at six thirty. Did she wait for her every evening? Oh no, today they'd made special arrangements. Ordinarily she'd be helping her mother at the Relais right now.

Herman put down his umbrella, pulled up a chair. The fleet-footed office girls came and went with the same vigorous gait as early that morning, never glancing their way, displaying, Herman understood, a professional conscientiousness that nothing could be allowed to distract. Charlotte studied the floor, her feet, seemingly impervious to boredom. Little wrinkles marked the corners of her mouth and eyes. With a slightly unwholesome compassion, Herman observed that beneath her loosely tied blouse her body was saggy for a young woman's, and she wasn't displaying it to its best advantage half sprawled out like that, with an indifference that bothered and saddened Herman. Again he felt a nagging desire to grab and shake her, to make her mouth divulge everything that was in her, everything she was, which he assumed to be incomprehensibly ordinary and flat but which, for that reason, he thought, would never stop goading his desire to know more, his curiosity and impatience—the more ordinary it was, he told himself, the less his longing would be satisfied, and the more his imagination would chase after what he dimly saw as the essence of Charlotte, perhaps still hidden to him alone. But she didn't seem like she'd ever had the desire or capacity to hide anything at all; she didn't seem as if she'd ever conceived of any reason for doing so.

Herman pulled his chair closer to Charlotte's, and she gave him a vague smile. Where exactly in the Relais did she live, if she didn't mind his asking? No, she didn't mind, room eleven, with the president, she'd been living there for three years. So she lived with Alfred? A little taken aback at Herman's surprise, Charlotte sweetly shrugged her shoulders.

With Alfred, yes, so she and Herman were neighbors, and besides room eleven was one of the best and most expensive in the hotel. Needless to say it was Alfred who paid for it. But Charlotte didn't have any ribbons? She let out an amused little chuckle.

"We're not married," she explained, "or engaged, so no, no ribbons in sight yet for me."

Suddenly her eyes were twinkling as if someone had told a good joke. Where had that come from, asked Herman, displeased, the idea of moving in with Alfred? Wasn't that a slightly odd way to live? Oh no, because Charlotte had had a room of her own for a very long time, until she was twenty-three or -four, on the second floor, overlooking the courtyard, but once her parents had needed it for an extra customer, and since they didn't know where to put Charlotte her mother suggested she move in with the president, who liked her and agreed right away, and who was away all day long in any case and didn't bother her at all. That was how her life with Alfred began. Charlotte had nothing to complain about. It worked out for everyone. Besides, wasn't she a little too grown up now to have a room all to herself, a room that could bring in money; even if, from another point of view, she did work at the Relais, to be sure, as hard as she could?

Herman snickered, and then, since the subject

angered and saddened him, he dropped it to ask about Gilbert, Charlotte's brother. He told her Gilbert had raised the possibility of a doubles match with the county councilor, but Herman wasn't inclined to accept.

Charlotte blushed slightly, and for the first time since the start of their conversation she turned to Herman and looked at him straight on. But the tone of her voice was unchanged, slightly leaden, apathetic. She made pronunciation mistakes that offended Herman's ears, however he tried to ignore them. He mustn't refuse, she was saying, because Gilbert would be hurt and there had to be a good reason why Gilbert wanted Herman as a partner, something to do with the way he'd been courting the district councilor for two or three years—it was time something came of that, and why shouldn't Herman help out if he could? Gilbert deserved it, Charlotte was convinced of that. And according to him when you live in such a remote village your only chance at bettering yourself is to climb onto the solid shoulders of some well-placed person, earning his goodwill and even making yourself—as Gilbert was doing with Lemaître—indispensable. No doubt the tennis match with Herman would put the crowning touch on certain specific efforts Gilbert had made, efforts whose nature Charlotte didn't know, but all along he'd shown a willingness to do many things to ingratiate himself with Lemaître, in a spirit of self-abnegation that Charlotte admired and supported, she herself having no ambition to pride herself on. Gilbert's willingness to do anything, yes, she admired that. His willingness, if necessary, to abandon all pride, respect for custom, decency, yes, she admired that too. Because she herself was far too weak and too stupid to set her mind on anything, that's just how it was.

And Charlotte went on in a flurry of banal truisms, deformed proverbs, and tired clichés that Herman was no longer listening to. He simply looked at her, frowning, unsatisfied. And with great difficulty he held back from touching her, groping her, pawing her in some way—pitying her and vaguely resenting her for it.

"What about Alfred?" he said. "What are you hoping for from him?"

But she couldn't think what she might hope for from anyone, because there was nothing she wanted. It was enough for her to help out by staying on at the Relais instead of moving to the Hôtel du Commerce, the village's other boarding house, where the prices were slightly lower. She had nothing to complain about. Everyone treated her well, particularly Alfred, who was very nice to share his room with her. Charlotte's mother didn't even give him a discount.

"You're not sharing his room," said Herman. "He took you in, that's all."

But Charlotte didn't understand these semantic subtleties. She shrugged, and her slightly weary face went even blanker than before. Doing nothing to hide it, she waited for Herman to change the subject or stop talking, and she too was capable of anything, although she hadn't chosen to be, and didn't realize that she was.

Finally, Métilde appeared, the last of thirty-some secretaries and office workers to come through the door. Emerging behind her, a man gently pushed her aside and hurried out into the street. He'd put on a rain hat, a yellow oilcloth hat, like a sailor's.

"Hey, the mayor," said Charlotte, dully.

"I have to see him!" Herman cried.

But he didn't even try to go after him. He was more eager to say hello to Métilde, to exchange a few words with her there in the lobby.

"I'll talk to him tomorrow," he said.

He thought informing the mayor of his situation was simply his duty, and he was no longer convinced the mayor would be shocked and take immediate, concrete steps to help him. In all honesty, he no longer even saw that as a possibility. Happily resigned, he told himself the village would decide his fate. But he didn't like people openly disregarding his case, and in a firm voice, meant to be heard by the two women, he added:

"Yes, tomorrow I'll talk to him, definitely."

He was happy to see that Métilde greeted his presence with visible pleasure and curiosity. She invited him to come along to her apartment for an aperitif. And her chignon was as perfectly smooth as it had been that morning, her cheeks dewy and fresh, her brow authoritarian and resolute. She brazenly grasped Charlotte's arm. In fact, she seemed to share Herman's irrepressible desire to handle her friend's flaccid body, because he saw her poking and kneading it with a sort of implacable ardor but no plausible pretext. She clasped Charlotte's waist as if to help her up, then clutched Charlotte's two hands in hers, then suddenly squeezed her shoulders and palpated the back of her neck with little sighs of hungry contentment, while Herman, envying her freedom to give Charlotte this unusual treatment, wondered what sort of agreement between them had accorded Métilde the privilege she was so casually exercising there in the lobby of the town hall, before the eyes of a stranger.

Charlotte did nothing to stop her. Suddenly annoyed, as if in a fit of frustration at some vague, repeated failure, Métilde let go of her friend and called to Herman:

"Let's go to my apartment. You can help me make her see sense."

And Charlotte let out a little giggle.

Soon they were in Métilde's room on the top floor of the bakers' house, for which she paid what Herman considered a vastly inflated fifteen hundred francs a month. But rooms to rent were scarce in the village. Having left the family farm some thirty kilometers away to come and work in the town hall, Métilde had been delighted by the bakers' price. Besides, as Herman understood it, no one saw anything contemptible—only the natural order of things—in the greed of the local merchants, highly regarded as they were for their influence over the mayor, for their network of contacts all over the region, even beyond L., and also perhaps for the indisputable majesty of the wives, whether straight and severe or gracefully bowed behind their counters, twelve hours a day— their grace was genuinely inexhaustible, unaffected by late-afternoon fatigue or miserly customers.

Herman was surprised to find Métilde's tidy little room filled with books. Everywhere he looked he saw works on accounting, manuals for word processing machines, self-taught courses in secretarial skills, treatises on marketing, all the many ways to self-improvement. Apart from that, there were only a few old pieces of furniture loaned by the bakers; the bed was draped with a comforter, the curtains were crocheted. Charlotte half reclined on the comforter, sighing with happiness.

"She's going to fall asleep," said Métilde.

She hurried forward to tug at Charlotte and sit her up on the edge of the bed. Charlotte frowned gently. But she obediently held the position Métilde had imposed on her, arms crossed over her thighs, mouth agape from dreaminess or exhaustion. As Métilde got out the bottles and glasses, scurrying from the sink to the armoire, she explained to Herman, in her crisp voice untouched by the slightest trace of weariness, that she'd been studying tirelessly for two years, all on her own, in hopes of one day finding work as an administrative assistant in L., because her ambition was not, absolutely not, to end up as a receptionist in the village town hall, or even a summer employee at the Chamber of Commerce; no, her ambition was to push herself, through work and will, all the way to L., where she'd set her sights on a number of businesses. She would soon take the exam for the Vocational Training Certificate, which meant going to L., sometime in April. She blushed a little as she spoke, and turned away in what Herman told himself was a blend of pride and trepidation.

He complimented her, but the sight of her books with their dry titles and cover photographs of determined, striving people filled him with a sudden exhaustion, as when Gilbert brought up the tennis match. He wished he could bury his nose in the comforter and its very discreet attic smell. But he was stirred by Métilde's intensity. Again he wished her immediate success.

"Oh yes," said Charlotte.

She was visibly forcing herself not to drop back on the mattress. Métilde poured glasses of fortified wine and sat down beside Charlotte. Again she explained to Herman what she'd meant earlier when she spoke of making Charlotte see sense. She meant nothing less than convincing her to give up the life she was leading, persuading her to follow in Métilde's own footsteps, who would gladly sacrifice all she had to support and guide her, to convince her to work toward a career, like Métilde, and to become at long last a free and accomplished person, far from the village, where pernicious influences kept her down. Charlotte, said Métilde, was by nature an undemanding and cooperative person, powerless to resist the machinations aiming to make her serve the most ignoble interests, and—worst of all—interests deeply counter to her own, which out of pure apathy she refused to see. But Métilde knew what Charlotte's best interests were. And so, bent toward Herman, her eye slightly fevered, she admitted unblinkingly that she would gladly renounce her ambitions if it meant she could give her friend a hand, as long as Charlotte committed to following her advice. Everything she'd read, everything she'd learned, all the efforts she'd made over the previous two years, she would happily offer it all up to Charlotte if she would only say at last that she was ready to receive her teaching, that it was long past time. She could quickly teach Charlotte the rudiments of secretarial work. Then she would help her study for her Vocational Training Certificate, which Métilde called the true key to a freedom no one had ever thought of giving Charlotte; a freedom she was too weak to demand, couldn't even imagine, a freedom that would blossom in the lively, hard-working life of an executive secretary, for instance, at the Bodin Marble Works in L., where Métilde knew the switchboard operator. And then, if Charlotte ever appeared in the village again, it would be at the wheel of her own car, and no one would ask anything of her; she would sleep in her own room and pay for everything with her own money. Such was Métilde's vision for Charlotte. And all her own successes meant nothing to her next to that.

Herman sipped gingerly at the slightly musty sweet wine. He nodded in agreement, enchanted by Métilde's rapturous, almost transparent face. It occurred to him that he might say, "I'm a teacher, maybe in Paris there's something I can do..." but he hesitated and missed his chance.

"I'm just fine the way I am," mumbled Charlotte.

"No, you're not," Métilde answered softly, sighing, "you're absolutely not."

She stroked Charlotte's head and said:

"Monsieur Herman, how can we get her to understand that she needs to make something of herself?"

Leafing through a manual on computer languages, he smiled awkwardly and shrugged with his elbows. Now and then the spattering rain on the windows half drowned out their voices. Encouraged by Métilde's full, smooth face, thinking he could trust her, he asked if she thought he was obliged to say yes to the tennis match with Gilbert against the district councilor.

PART TWO

1 – Herman would pass by the inevitably wide-open door to Alfred's room, shared by Charlotte, and see the bed strewn with the cassettes she listened to whenever she had a free moment, and magazines devoted to cooking or scandals involving people whose names meant nothing to Herman but were well known to Charlotte, which she read with a passion that—Herman grumpily told himself—she never threw into anything else. Charlotte would get up very early to bring the president his breakfast, and often he would criticize what she brought him; he was always out of sorts in the morning. Then he would leave for work at the town hall and Charlotte would set about cleaning the rooms, giving Herman no chance to approach her like he wished he could: she worked with great diligence, fearing her mother, and although she never said it to his face she didn't like him even simply asking a question that would

force her to turn off the vacuum to hear, or pause as she scrubbed out a sink or swatted a bedspread. Any other time of day, the mother would have urged Charlotte to talk with Herman for as long as he liked. But during housekeeping hours she'd come creeping up, stand behind Herman, smiling, affable, and assign Charlotte some task or other—keeping her eyes on her—in a voice that Herman found nothing short of exquisite in spite of himself. And, since he hadn't yet talked to her about the exorbitant price of his board and didn't feel at ease in her presence, he'd soon wander off, slowly, regretfully. He went back to his room, glancing toward the window. The rain poured down, erasing the hills in the distance. Sometimes, with the skies so gray and the clouds so low, he couldn't even see the face of the old woman across the way, but he no longer minded being watched. Because was there ever anything strange or private in his behavior? The whole village could have had their eyes glued to him twenty-four hours a day, watching his every move, and they would have nodded their heads with un-wavering approval.

Then, having nothing else to do, he would take a little nap. He would also sometimes walk past Gilbert's room, but quickly, staring straight ahead. And if he sensed that Gilbert was there, lying on his bed, smoking, then he would race to the toilets at the end of the hall and lock himself in until Gilbert was gone.

Sometimes the father would happen upon Herman and, to make conversation, tell him with a sigh:

"Our Gilbert's out of work, it's been more than two years, what hope do we have of finding something for him in the village?"

And the mother would chime in:

"It's sad, seeing him hang around here all the time with nothing to do. At least he has his weekend connections in L., something's going to come of that, I'm sure of it."

But the parents, proud of their son's handsome face, didn't want him to be offered a position as some sort of subordinate. They wanted to see him in business school, and they were indignant that it required a *baccalauréat*, which Gilbert didn't have. And so they'd staked their pride on seeing to it that he got in without one, through the intercession of his friend Lemaître, an important figure in L. They also seemed to have gotten the idea that Herman was somehow going to help Gilbert get on his feet, although they hadn't heard about the tennis match. They lavished him with kindness and attention, particularly the mother, but Herman was still resolved to pay only half of what they were asking when the end of the month came. Which was why he avoided her, despite the captivating courtesies she was capable of dispensing.

All day long he would wander around the hotel, heading aimlessly upstairs, then down, trying to bump into Charlotte, hiding from Gilbert and the mother. He ceremoniously greeted any other guests he met, and they him. They were mostly traveling salesmen. The rain and the cold discouraged any thought of going out. And with Charlotte he had the emptiest conversations over and over, never unhappy about it, adapting to the simple way her thoughts progressed, affectionately squeezing a bit of her flesh here or there. Charlotte's tranquil existence was filled with housekeeping, magazines, and serving the ever capricious and demanding president, Alfred. How could she need anything more? Indifferent to her appearance, she always dressed in the same unbecoming clothes.

"She charms the worst part of me," mused Herman, "the laziest part, the most shiftless. The hours go by without thought or vitality, and everything's the same, from minor villainies to virtuous good deeds. How restful, yes, what a restful life this is! What a restful place is this village!"

At six thirty, he would rouse himself and go wait for Métilde in the lobby of the town hall. They drank a glass of fortified wine at her apartment, all the while discussing Métilde's chances of success, as well as the possibility of saving Charlotte, which interested Herman less, because he didn't believe anyone could or should extract her from her torpor. Dynamic tension kept Métilde's shoulders straight and square. And although he was very fond of her, a growing weariness made Herman less talkative around Métilde every day.

"The Bodin Marble Works, the Vocational Training Certificate, all that fuss and work day after day, what's the point?" he vaguely asked himself. "Who cares?"

He wasn't far from thinking that a rudimentary, inert existence in the hibernating village was the only life worth living. But he still forced himself to believe that—with her pure, honest, industrious will—Métilde brought out all his finest instincts, that her presence was good for him, as the unconsciously toxic Charlotte's was not. He paged through Métilde's books, did his best to provide useful advice. He would have been happier sprawled on the comforter; he would gladly have lain there silent and mindless for hours on end.

Then Gilbert, Métilde's long-time lover, would show up, pouring himself generous glasses of port and holding forth, perpetually upbeat and confident.

Gilbert and Métilde would talk about leaving the village for the bustling subprefecture city of L., Gilbert smugly depicting his life as a student admitted to the First School of Business with no baccalauréat, while in a few hopeful words Métilde modestly evoked an executive secretary position at the Bodin Marble Works, then gave up even on that, not wanting to even think of leaving before she'd saved Charlotte from her pointlessness.

"Yes, life in this village is a good life to live," thought Herman, "once summer's over there's nothing to do with yourself, and boredom without awareness or resentment slows the mind, and the subprefecture city of L. seems unreachable in the storms: you have to accept it, and even deep in an ugly little room with flowered wallpaper, find your way to restfulness, to a sort of dulled, larval inertia. Such a good life!"

All the same, he took care not to interrupt Gilbert and Métilde as, more and more heated, their voices sharp and seething, they went on and on about the village, suddenly scorned amid their evocations of L.'s superiority. In the village, Gilbert couldn't enjoy or exploit his prerogatives as a universally charming young man. In the village, Métilde couldn't rise professionally, she could learn only the theory of a life enriched and liberated by a very modern career, which in her eyes was perfectly represented by the vision of herself entering the Bodin company's receipts and expenses into a computer. In the village, Métilde had no prospects but ribbons for her blouse and everything that came with them. She wanted no such life, she said, for her dear Charlotte either.

"Oh, why not?" thought Herman, submerged in his deep lethargy.

Tired of this talk, he abruptly changed the subject to his missing family, and asked what might become of them and of himself. To his own surprise, he was racked by a dry sob. But could he even quite remember what Rose and the boy looked like? He could not—little more than their first names. He could very precisely picture the vague, indifferent expression that sometimes dulled Métilde's eyes, he knew everything down to the exact tone of the dismissive little "oh" that would escape Gilbert's suddenly slack lips.

"What has to happen will happen," one or the other of them would invariably say.

They showed no sign of discomfort, at most mild surprise that Herman was revisiting a closed subject, with what might have struck them as a sort of impropriety.

"Alfred wouldn't be happy with me," Herman would tell himself.

Nonetheless, just once, Métilde let slip a word that Herman turned over and over in his mind without quite managing to connect it to his problem, though his problem was precisely what she was talking about. She said something about the many avatars in this damp region. Gilbert yawned, so Métilde dutifully perked up and announced that the local want ads were always asking for people with the Vocational Training Certificate, and once you had that in your hand, no, you'd have no problem finding a job in L. that paid eight thousand francs after taxes.

Herman choked down the rest of his wine and said his goodbyes. Through his weariness, he was grateful to Métilde for enlivening the past hour with her cheerful chatter and the pretty sight of her cheeks pinkening with every mention of the Vocational Training Certificate, etc.

Later, beneath his umbrella, his thoughts turned to the avatars, but focused, sustained reflection was growing hard for him, as he had so few occasions to practice it. He caught himself daydreaming or vacantly gazing at the dark shop windows, imagining the merchant women at home, wondering if among family they permitted themselves to liberate their customarily compressed and flattened breasts just a little. After eight, the streets were deserted. Low, narrow windows between the timbers, dim lights, not a sound filtering out, not even a television. Herman hurried to the Relais, almost embarrassed at the thought of being seen outside at that hour.

"Ah, I was waiting for you," Alfred always said, sitting on Herman's bed, ten minutes after dinner was done.

"I stopped by Métilde's," Herman would answer.

But Alfred knew every move he made, like everyone in the village, Herman supposed. And so—though as time went by he found it less and less disagreeable, more and more inoffensive—he had to endure the assault of Alfred's impetuous friendship, his eagerness to hear Herman tell him he was happy and felt himself becoming a genuine villager who didn't miss Paris at all in spite of the constant rain, and the little there was to do, and the solid gray sky masking the hills on all sides. And once Herman obediently acknowledged his contentment and the relative tranquility of his mind, Alfred would triumphantly promise he'd be reunited with Rose and the child, possibly soon— although he himself couldn't say—but when he did, the meeting might not bring him any more joy than he would feel next summer, when, in the streets of the village they had only come to for shopping (for lavish, impulsive grocery purchases), he would once again see all the Parisian vacationers. The wife and the child would remind him of life in the capital, and Alfred was convinced that Herman would in fact look away, out of boredom and disgust with that existence.

"Well, why not?" thought Herman, trying to make out the face of the old woman across the way, the mother of the present charcutière.

The president's prediction no longer offended him, scarcely interested him. Now he knew Alfred dyed or bleached his hair to match the intense blondness around him, since his eyebrows were still black and thick, like the hairs that darkened his wrists and upper hands. Out of pure affection for Herman, Alfred regularly offered to have Charlotte serve him breakfast, as she did his, at no added expense.

"No, no, never," Herman would answer, feeling the burden of Alfred's solicitude, Alfred's eagerness to see him make full use of Charlotte like he did, and for the sake of Herman's comfort and pleasure, Alfred would be perfectly prepared to secretly pay off the mother for Charlotte's added labor.

"And why would he do that?" Herman limply asked himself.

Because he was trying to keep him there in the village, to keep him rhapsodizing several times a day over the excellent life to be had here, but Herman didn't need Alfred, didn't need Alfred's devoted attention to the perfect repose of his soul, to feel a gratitude toward the off-season village for what it was giving him—a progressive indifference to action and mental labor—and so Herman, idle and drowsing, his half-closed eyes vaguely registering the pretentious little flowers interlaced on the ceiling, came to think that vitality is in no way a necessity, nor is a certain sort of happiness made up of varied activities, heartfelt affections, and a comfortable, discreet wealth, like he'd known until recently with Rose in the fourteenth arrondissement of Paris. But neither did he want that Parisian life to be taken away from him, he felt no contempt for it. It was just that, for the moment, he was powerfully drawn to the possibility of an indolent but not ignoble, serenely oblivious degeneration. Charlotte didn't think she had to be saved, but was she right? Nothing was less certain, but he felt his friendship for her growing.

2 – With Métilde's intercession, he'd gotten his name on the list for an audience with the mayor, having accepted that he had to wait his turn. And now a meeting had been scheduled, and the day had come. He wearily made his way to the town hall, no longer convinced that his problem deserved a place among the cases requiring urgent attention. Hadn't they already made it very clear that his situation was of no particular interest? He gave his name at the front desk, then climbed the stairs alone to the mayor's

office, which occupied the whole second floor. There he had to identify himself to another secretary, who would verify the rationale behind his request for an interview and usher him in when the time came. Herman recognized her immediately: she was his one-time neighbor on the plateau, the farmwoman, the first person he'd gone to see to ask about Rose. She gave him a wide, detached smile and in a precise voice told him she knew why he'd come to see the mayor and in all honesty didn't think it was sufficient grounds to disturb him, but she would let Herman in all the same, taking into account the friendships he'd made in this very building, among the employees.

"So you don't work at the farm anymore?" asked Herman, for whom this reunion was not a pleasant one.

He remembered losing his composure in front of her, and he was ashamed.

"When the cold weather comes I switch to the town hall," she explained laconically.

Then she stood up to open the mayor's door, announced, "Monsieur Herman," and with a graceful one-handed wave showed him in.

It was an enormous room of ultramodern décor, exactly like downstairs. The mayor was sitting at a large desk made of a single plate of glass, no papers or pencils before him. But his serious air and stern posture made an impression on Herman, who forced himself to shake off his apathy.

"I know everything I have to know about your case," the mayor said with a smile. "What I don't know is what you're hoping for from me."

Herman simply wanted to introduce himself to the leading figure in the village; to make sure his case was known; in short, to take the steps required by the most basic rules of civic life: he told him that. At the same time, if the mayor had any thoughts on his problem, he would be glad to hear them. And he sat down facing him on a metal chair, his thighs, like the mayor's, slightly magnified and deformed through the desk's glass. The mayor sighed, as if steeling himself to say something unpleasant. And what follows he threw out all at one go, not looking at Herman, but still maintaining the slightly precious, affable, congenial air he would never have dreamed of abandoning, even if he could. It was obvious, he declared, obvious indeed to everyone here—Alfred included, no matter what he might have told Herman—that Herman would never again see his wife and his child as he knew them, in their customary, untransfigured form, speaking as they spoke in their ordinary lives. No, Herman had to renounce all hope of ever again seeing his wife and his child that way. This had happened before, and it was the same every time.

Nothing set Herman's case apart from the others. No one here felt any surprise at what had befallen him, much less troubled themselves over it for long, and when they saw the missing pair on the village streets or, who knows, on the roads in the hills, they would simply say hello to them, without fear or surprise or any particular joy. They might not even bother to tell Herman. Because there was nothing at all interesting about it, in any real sense.

"But, I mean, will they be alive?" asked Herman, his voice shaking a little.

"In a way," answered the mayor.

He looked at his watch. Herman understood that the time set aside for this meeting was strictly limited. He realized that he shouldn't try to eat into the time allotted to the next hopeful, that he should be satisfied with whatever he was told and stay patient and polite.

"In a way," the mayor repeated.

As if doing Herman a great favor, he explained: They would be alive, but only in the manner of the woman who peers into the Relais, whom Alfred must have told Herman was "the mother of the present charcutière." What Alfred didn't say, and what the mayor now allowed himself to divulge on the theory that Herman wouldn't have gone much longer not knowing it, is that in all likelihood the face belonged to Alfred's wife, who'd come with him for a vacation in the village fourteen years before and had never been seen again, except in her current role and her current setting, smiling and peering at the rear façade of the Relais day and night from a tiny window that was indeed located over the charcuterie, in what must be an uninhabited room, a sort of storage area, in the charcutiers' apartment. But no one could see any point in asking questions about that room. Pleasant, never intrusive, that face, that being had chosen to settle in with them. She always behaved herself and knew the ways of the village, which is all that mattered. Some of the villagers recognized her as Alfred's wife—he'd reported her disappearance way back when—and then she appeared at the window three weeks afterward, fresh and discreet. Who would ever have thought of even mentioning it to Alfred? He'd rather not have it spread around that it was his wife, his wife's face. He had every right. Everyone understood his reticence. But they knew the truth. But they didn't bother themselves with that truth in any way. Now and then—rarely—someone spotted Alfred's vanished wife in the village, on the main square. They said hello to her, kept walking, nothing more.

"Does she answer?" asked Herman.

No, of course not. Didn't Herman understand, asked the mayor in surprise, that he was talking about emanations, not people? About visible, gracious souls, not bodies and minds?

Herman let out a little laugh. An awkward silence ensued. Although clearly bored with the discussion of things that ordinarily needed no explaining, the mayor seemed politely insistent on telling Herman everything he knew, as if, thought Herman, he was a villager now, and had to be taught.

"And why does what happens happen?" Herman asked meekly.

A brief flash of gratification further brightened the mayor's almost transparent eyes. He couldn't tell him anything certain, but his opinion was this: in the cases he knew best, though Herman's wasn't yet among them, one of the spouses felt an insurmountable repulsion when it came time to start back to Paris on the thirty-first of August. On one pretext or another, that person got away from the house, set off into the countryside or came down to the village in the no doubt half-aware hope that something would happen to prevent the return. Their distress in that moment, thought the mayor, must have been intense. And then they were seen again some time later, in the airy form Herman had observed in Alfred's wife, and—most importantly—bound for all time to the village. The abandoned wife or husband generally stayed. Some left for home, but the stubborn soul never did go back to Paris. It settled into the village or in some quiet spot on the plateau; it showed itself or it didn't. Those beings' personalities varied. They were never a nuisance—yes, people were fond of them. And they're so discreet, why get hung up on them? The mayor assured Herman that people forgot about them like they forgot about the rain, like they forgot about the stones and the grass by the roadsides.

"Is it really because they suddenly can't stand the thought of Paris?" asked Herman. "Why would that be?"

"I have no idea, I don't know Paris," said the mayor.

He added that, in his opinion, the repugnance for Paris and the longing to stay that transformed those afflicted with what he called village sickness into pure evanescences might, without either one's knowing it, have met a similar repugnance and a similar longing, only a little less powerful, in the other partner, who for that reason adapted without difficulty to the new state of affairs, and, like Alfred, no longer seriously considered trying to change it. Who knows, the mayor went on with a sly smile, maybe Alfred had endeavored to inspire that illness in his wife, not having the courage and will to enter the floating state himself? But the souls were happy— the mayor could assure Herman of that. They had what they'd pined for as captives of the practical world: an eternal, peaceful existence in the village, a knowledge of the off-season far from Paris, and the constant rain, and the comfort it brings. Gloating, the mayor asked:

"Have you noticed, Monsieur Herman, you can't even see the hills anymore! By the eighth or ninth of September the horizon disappears, everything's gray; this is nowhere, we're in the very middle of nowhere!"

Seeing Herman smile but make no reply, he added by way of conclusion that if all this interested him he had only to wait for the gliding, impalpable forms of Rose and the little boy to appear, though they might very well stay hidden. He said again that he thought he recognized Herman as one of those husbands who wouldn't be going home.

"Oh, I don't know about that," Herman protested weakly.

If he did stay, and if he needed money, the mayor could find him work giving math lessons to the shopkeepers' children—private lessons being greatly sought-after in the village at the moment, primarily for the touch of prestige they conferred.

"For now, I'd just like to withdraw some money from the bank," said Herman.

"Then ask Gilbert to drive you to L."

The mayor stood up. He probably knew the details

of Herman's life in the village better than Herman did himself.

Back at the hotel, as Herman lay stretched out on the bed, drifting off to sleep, Charlotte's mother came to tell him he was wanted on the telephone downstairs. He went down in his stocking feet, as he inevitably did in the Relais now, lacking the initiative to put on his shoes.

It was the principal of the Parisian high school where Herman had been teaching for nearly twenty years. Herman listened in contrite silence as the principal complained about the difficulties he'd had getting ahold of him. It was a little after ten o'clock. Herman heard recess sounds on the other end of the line. A little surge of nostalgia made him tighten his grip on the receiver, absorbed in his thoughts. They were worried; they'd been surprised not to see him there on the first day of class. What were they supposed to think, what decision should they make? Herman wearily explained that he couldn't possibly consider going back to work until he'd seen Rose and the child, which the principal entirely understood, his tone turning grave and respectful. He was aware of Herman's case, thanks to a brief story from the local press reprinted in a Paris newspaper. It was known in Paris that such things happened, and the principal was deeply sorry, but not shocked. He simply hoped

Herman would be home before they were forced to find a replacement for him. He offered his condolences. And when, with a little laugh, Herman refused them, the principal didn't back down, defending the opinion of the newspaper he'd read, which said people who disappeared there disappeared forever.

"That's not exactly what they told me," Herman asserted.

But the principal was sure of his information, although that was as much as he knew: no family thus separated had ever been reunited.

"Well, we'll see," said Herman, breezily.

And he shivered with relief as he heard the end-of-recess bell ring back in Paris. He was so happy to be standing in his socks in the Relais's silent dining room, observed and spied on by Charlotte's mother, to be sure, and robbed of any opportunity to be completely alone, but, he reflected, since he never had to deal with anyone who thought like he did, as his Parisian friends and colleagues did, strangely delivered of the obligation to keep up a dignified appearance.

3 – Two or three days later, just before dinnertime, Herman was coming home from Métilde's, where

they'd examined a pamphlet she'd gotten on the career opportunities offered by a Vocational Training Certificate. With Gilbert not there and both of them sitting on the bed, she'd taken the opportunity to vigorously press her body to Herman's.

"I'm bothering you," she'd said sadly, as Herman sat stock still.

He was simply a little afraid of Gilbert, now that it had been agreed he'd be taking Herman to L., but he didn't dare admit it to Métilde, who sighed, turning away. In profile, he saw her nose turn red. And so his mood was downcast when he left her.

Out on the main street, he didn't immediately open his umbrella. The cold was sharper than the day before, and he thought there would be a freeze that night, the rain had become a fine drizzle. And then, as if they'd just come out of the closed housewares store on the corner of the main street and the square, he saw Rose and the little one, hand in hand. They came toward him, bareheaded, in the same summer clothes they were wearing three weeks ago. Like Herman's, their hair was dripping, and Rose's short skirt clung to her thighs. The boy looked terribly thin, and his T-shirt was plastered to his ribs. Herman stood frozen in terror. Why was he afraid? In spite of the cold, neither Rose nor the child trembled. There was nothing unusual about the look on their faces: it was peaceful, a little misty, but not so changed that Herman had any reason to be petrified. And yet he was. The umbrella fell to the ground and rolled into the gutter. Rose looked at him and smiled as they strolled past. It was a distant, impersonal gaze, a polite smile, nothing more. The sidewalk wasn't wide, and Herman thought Rose's arm had to have brushed against his. But he hadn't felt it—he was in fact sure there'd been no real physical contact. With great difficulty, he forced himself to turn around, and—relieved but still shivering—he watched them walk off, quickly, lightly, with eminently graceful steps. It almost seemed that the boy's slender legs were being moved by strings, delicately pulled to make him look as if he were dancing. Shouldn't Herman catch up with them and take them in his arms? It was only his fear of Gilbert that had stopped him from going to bed with Métilde a while ago, and so perhaps this meeting with Rose filled him with guilt, however convinced he was that she couldn't possibly know.

He forced himself to follow them all the same. In a tiny little voice, he even called out:

"Hey, Rose!"

But he was glad to see that she didn't turn around. They soon stopped at the window of the shoe store, and Rose seemed to reach for the door. Before Herman could see the door open they went in, disappeared into the dark shop, and if the door had opened, it was now closed again. Nothing was moving on the main street. No light filtered from the windows of the shoe shop. Herman didn't hear a sound, not even the rain, which his ears had grown used to and no longer noticed, by day or by night.

He hurried back to the Relais, but he didn't dare speak of what he'd seen to Alfred. He'd already noticed that the president walked with a perfectly relaxed gait back and forth in front of his window, in front of the attentive, ever benevolent gaze of the form across the way, sometimes glancing toward the glass—never speaking of the face, but never avoiding it either.

But the next morning Herman went back to the shoe store.

"If Rose did recognize me," he asked himself, "what must she have thought?"

Now he was thinking he could make up for his behavior the evening before by showing Rose he had been looking for her. He stood for a moment at the rain-blind window. The shop sold nothing but slippers, espadrilles, and rubber boots. He was afraid to go in, terrified at the idea of seeing Rose again. The shopkeeper welcomed him into the empty store with the wide, charming, cold smile Herman was now so used to seeing in the village, which he sensed he was slowly coming to imitate, showing his teeth more than he ever did before, ducking his head until his chin almost touched his chest, and so peering up in an involuntarily cajoling way. Severely confined by her blouse, the woman's breath was labored and loud. Her face was deep red from the tightly pulled cords, her posture was unnaturally straight, and she often put her hand to her chest as if asking its forgiveness for what she was forcing it to endure. Ill at ease, Herman tried hard to seem relaxed. He wandered around the shop for a moment, then asked, too abruptly: did she have any rooms that weren't occupied by the house's inhabitants?

"Yes, we have two or three empty bedrooms," she graciously answered, and she nodded once, twice, although every move left her even more short of breath. Pulled up into a chignon, her hair was so pale and fine that Herman began to wonder if it was indeed a physical substance and not a sort of halo, discreetly ordinary in its appearance, but a halo all the same.

"And is it possible," Herman went on, "is it possible that there's someone living in one of those rooms at the moment?"

"Of course, there might be. Who can ever be sure there isn't? At the moment," the woman assured him, "I wouldn't be surprised."

She laughed a little, vaguely flirtatious. But Herman sensed she was taking particular care to put on a charming, carefree face because she wasn't happy with his questions. He realized he shouldn't have forced her to speak of her permanent tenants, who were obviously well known to everyone. Still, didn't he have every right to seek some confirmation of what he'd felt upon running into Rose the evening before?

And now, at the hotel, Alfred was taking him to task for his behavior with the woman in the shoe shop, having heard of it even before Herman came back. Herman had committed a grave offense against good taste, said Alfred. He must never again question any villager on those phenomena; there was nothing remotely interesting about them. Then he smiled, triumphant:

"Didn't I tell you you'd see them again?"

"But I want to talk to them," said Herman.

"That's impossible, they're not going to answer you, that's just how it is. And why bother them? From this point forward," Alfred said solemnly, "you must try to be as perfectly happy in the village as they are in their eternal drifting—without cares, without ambitions, free of any binding relationship."

He lowered his voice. He was standing in Herman's room with his back to the window, but

Herman could see that the face across the way never took its eyes off him.

"We just have to stay, don't you agree, it would be too terrible to abandon them," Alfred whispered, his eyes damp.

4 – The days went by in the village, Herman no longer troubling to determine the date. Lying on his bed, hands clasped behind his neck, he watched the comings and goings through his open door, and that was all that occupied him for the day. When Charlotte went by he sat up, called out to her, and they exchanged a few words about the rain. Now he wished he'd accepted Alfred's offer to have Charlotte serve him his breakfast. But ever since his meeting with Rose and the child, ever since he'd learned that they'd both taken up residence in the village, he'd noticed that Alfred seemed less bent on convincing him to stay, clearly thinking the matter was settled, so Herman feared that Charlotte's services would end up on his bill rather than Alfred's as Alfred had first suggested, back, as Herman remembered, when Alfred still had some reason to fear he might go home to Paris. And out of pure laziness Herman still hadn't challenged the absurdly high rate he was being charged for his

bed and board. He could easily imagine Charlotte's mother asking an outrageous price for her daughter's attentions. With calculated regularity she bemoaned the fact that she was still supporting her two adult children, deploring the dearth of career opportunities in the village, grimly portraying herself as ruined through the fault of those two jobless young people. And she strongly encouraged any contacts or connections they might forge here or there—Charlotte at the Relais, Gilbert on his excursions to the subprefecture—so strongly that it would have been difficult to break them off without her permission. She had, according to Alfred who didn't trust her, the typical mindset of a village merchant.

She came looking for Herman, greeted him with a deep bow, and said:

"They're holding the annual merchants' dinner tonight, at the charcuterie, around eight o'clock. Would you do us the honor of joining us, dear Monsieur Herman?"

Still lying on his bed, he vaguely lifted his head and asked if the owner of the shoe store would be there.

"Of course, every shopkeeper, hotelier, and café owner in the village will be there, and so will the mayor. You'll be a special guest, we'd so like to have you," Charlotte's mother purred.

She slipped out, certain of Herman's consent, and her espadrilles slapped lazily down the stairs, a little sound now familiar and dear to Herman's ear, like the sound of the rain.

That evening, he had to walk only a few steps to reach the neighboring charcuterie. Charlotte had pressed his one suit, a linen suit he'd been wearing since summer. He'd shaved for the occasion, and trimmed the hair on the back of his neck. He was excited by the invitation, but apprehensive. This, he understood, was an exceptional honor they were granting him, seeking his presence at a gathering to which only merchants were called. He believed they were even allowing the mayor a privilege that was in no way automatic, about which he had every reason to be flattered, mayor though he be. And he, Herman, a former Parisian, had earned this honor by his rigorously appropriate attitude, and also no doubt by his presumed ability to offer invaluable services of some sort—as a teacher full of wise counsel—even if at the moment he wasn't working, and regularly showed himself in the most slovenly attire.

He opened the door to the closed shop, the little bells tinkling overhead. The charcutière immediately appeared and led him up the traditional narrow, winding staircase to the second floor. The other guests were already there, she told him, and Herman saw her

tall mass of tightly bound, nearly white hair dimly lu-
minescing in the darkness. He nervously stepped into
the dining room, where a long table of twenty-five or
thirty places had been set, and hurried to sit in the
seat pointed out by his hostess, between Charlotte's
mother and the head of the village real-estate agency.
The room was small and low-ceilinged, as was usual
in houses in the center of the village, darkened by
thick beams and meagerly windowed. The table completely filled the room, which was lit only by a floor
lamp in the corner, so it took Herman some time to
make out his tablemates' faces. A fire was crackling
in the oversized fireplace just behind the couple who
ran the antique shop, both of them peering down
their noses. The rain slapped the windowpanes, and
the two satellite dishes recently installed on a slope of
the roof knocked together in the furious wind.

Herman sat hunched on his chair, soaking wet.
He was afraid he might not prove worthy of the
honor they were paying him, not knowing what arti-
cle of the code he should rely on here with the merchants—if he was supposed to jump straight into the
conversation or wait to be spoken to. A faint whiff of
mildew emanated from the woodwork, the old plaster.

"So my wife and son live in those people's house,"
thought Herman, troubled. "But how do they feel
about having them there?"

He was sitting across from the shoe sellers. Did they have any idea who he was? Everyone in the village knew, but these two gave no sign that they realized they were sitting across from the closest relative of their eternal and possibly unwelcome guests.

"Are they going to charge me rent?" Herman wondered. "And what made Rose choose their house specifically?"

He looked back and forth from the man to the woman, trying to catch an eye, looking for some sign of complicity, a little nod to say, "Yes, they're with us, come and see them, come see for yourself that they're with us and they're happy, and then why shouldn't they talk to you, why wouldn't they say something to you of all people?"

But when their eyes met Herman's they were lit only by the brief glint of sociable, ritual acknowledgment that people here offered everyone. Sitting down at the table, Herman had given the same glance to each of the guests, along with a nod, even though he couldn't yet quite see them. The tobacconists were there, and the director of the savings bank, the managers of the Co-op, the café and hotel owners, the two female pharmacists, the woman who ran the driving school, bakers, butchers, etc., and the mayor himself, sitting across the table not far from Herman, rather like him, Herman suddenly realized, in that they were both oddly sallow, slouching, shivering, and their hair was damp, the mayor's indisputably lighter but of a redder blond, a less extraordinarily pallid blond than everyone else's. And it struck Herman that like Alfred the mayor might dye his hair. Neither the mayor nor Herman sat up straight on his chair. The cold water hammering the windows seemed to physically lash them, and they were humbly bowing, defeated by the water, by the cold, by the fury of the driving rain. A drip hung perennially from Herman's nose. Who would ever have thought, seeing the mayor so crumpled and trembling, that he held the administration of the whole village in his hand? His tablemates were sitting up straight and serene, the women bound tight, breasts flattened, shoulders high and padded, the flesh of their arms bulging pink and full from beneath the elastic of their short sleeves. Their brows were pale and shiny. Their tranquil blue-tinged gaze still troubled Herman with its coldness and coquetry.

"How well these people stand up to the weather," Herman said to himself, gripped with fear and slightly ashamed of his own debilitation. Sitting next to him, the enormous, wan real-estate agent leaned over and whispered in his ear:

"That house of yours on the plateau, I might be able to help you unload it. Why don't you stop by the agency and see me?"

He smelled of sweat, to Herman's surprise and admiration, he who never perspired now.

"Yes," said Herman, "I might want to sell it."

"Oh, it's not going to be snapped up just like that, I don't know what we'll get for it, could be a pittance," the other man hastened to add.

But Herman only shrugged; it made no difference to him. Aperitifs had been served, and he realized that the talk had turned to local affairs, which the merchants seemed to consider it their duty to deal with. The baker jotted down the suggested solutions in a notebook. Everyone spoke in calm, quiet tones. Only Herman and the mayor stretched their necks to hear, and even then Herman could make out nothing more than an occasional snippet. They were discussing a family whose three children had to be removed at once from the dangerous influence of their alcoholic, depraved parents. The woman who ran the gift shop earnestly offered her testimony: Those people had bought two pornographic videos from her in two weeks. Worse—added the fishmonger who'd seen this as he passed by their window one evening—they watched them as a family, right in front of the children, all of them sitting around the kitchen table just after dinner, and the parents drank like it was a contest, and the father got so red and so agitated that the worst was to be feared.

"Well," said the gift shop owner, "I won't sell to them anymore."

They didn't have a car, so they couldn't go to L. in search of more films. They would simply have to be watched to be sure they didn't order them through the mail. The postman could be questioned. They turned next to the matter of a banishment from the village. Some young man, renting from the real-estate agent for two thousand francs a month, who'd moved here from a neighboring village to do summer work for the Parisians (gardening, running errands), now found himself without work or money. He'd stopped paying his rent, complaining it was too high. The real-estate agent wanted to be rid of him. After a brief deliberation, it was decided, as Herman understood it, that the young man would be expelled from the village. The owner of the Café du Commerce, the barber, and Charlotte's father would go wake him at dawn, immobilize him, drive him some twenty kilometers from the village, and forbid him to come back. There had been four such banishments in ten years, all successful, always involving recent arrivals who thought they could dig themselves out of dire financial straits by protesting the prices charged in the village.

"We don't put up with that here," said the real-estate agent in Herman's ear.

He rolled up his shirtsleeves, puffing loudly. Meanwhile, Herman couldn't get warm. He thought he could feel his waterlogged brain dripping onto the walls of his skull, water trickling all through his body with nowhere to drain. He was comforted to see that the mayor had crossed his arms over his chest in hopes of warming himself a little.

"There's one more case to settle," said the baker, who had already filled up several pages in her notebook.

Then:

"This is a delicate matter."

She'd learned from the social worker that the V. girl, thirteen, was accusing her stepfather of regular, routine violations of her person. He thought he had every right, he scarcely even tried to hide it.

"So you understand, this is about V.," said the baker woman after a silence.

And Herman had the impression that for some unspoken reason his tablemates were reluctant to take action against this V., whatever misdeeds he might be guilty of. The grocer sighed and promised he'd deal with it; his daughter knew the V. girl well. Relieved, the baker woman closed her notebook. Vol-au-vents and platters of charcuterie were brought in.

"The fire is bright, the flames are leaping, but it only warms the antiquarians' backs, it's so cold in here, so damp!" Herman said to himself.

Now he was afraid staying to the end of the meal might take a serious toll on him. His nostrils were stinging from the smell of mildew and must. Suddenly the door opened and someone quietly came in. It was the form, the being who had been peering at Herman since his first day at the Relais; it was Alfred's vanished wife, now living in the charcutiers' house. She was wearing an old-fashioned floral print summer dress. Smiling and silent, she glided all around the table, gently passed behind Herman, bowing right and left, infinitely amiable, the little sandals on her feet scarcely touching the ground—they whisked over it like a breeze. Seeing her up close for the first time, Herman thought she looked sad and tired beneath her endless smiles; she seemed old before her time. Troubled, anxious, he realized that no matter what he'd heard about these beings' ineffable happiness she was a lost soul, and, behind her little window all day long, the very image of boredom and despair.

Every guest gave her a quick nod, then paid her no further attention, though she went right on smiling and curtseying.

"Why," Herman wondered, bothered by their dismissiveness, "why did she want to stay on here, why didn't she go home to Paris? They—yes, that's it exactly—they don't even care that she's here, they don't see anything sacred about her, any more than a live-in maid."

Herman thought he felt the being touch him on the shoulder as she passed by. He didn't dare smile at her or look at her any longer than the others. But he felt like his heart was seeping and withering. The smell of the room now mingled with his disgust at the very fleshly odor of the real-estate agent, who sweated abundantly as he ate. Someone complained that the Parisians hadn't brought in as much money this year as the summers before. They hemmed and hawed before they bought anything of any value, the antiquarians groused. Yes, it was the same at the charcuterie, they'd bought far fewer terrines of this or that.

A painful compassion clenched Herman's throat, and as he looked at the woman he felt certain that the delicate, undulating silhouettes of Rose and the child that he'd glimpsed a week or two before only seemed to be happy, that their pale, serene, detached, smiling faces hid an inconsolable sorrow. Alfred's wife went on strolling around the table, she couldn't bring herself to leave. Her smile grew brighter and wider as she inspired ever more indifference among the dinner guests, who at the moment were intently calculating (the baker had gotten out her notebook again) how much pork, how much beef, poultry, and fish the Parisians had ingested this summer compared to last. One thing was certain: they'd eaten less than usual. There was worry in the air—suppose that trend continued?

"Rose wanted to stay," Herman mused, "she wanted to spend all eternity in the village, but if that turns out to have been a mistake, she still won't be going home, or me either. This is where we're from now, but how to get used to the water? The mayor and I are literally liquefying, I can see it, our flesh going spongy, we'll never have the fine strong build that people have around here, the dry hair, the skin beaded with sweat. And yet I've got to stay, I've got to make a place for myself here."

Finally, Alfred's wife left the room, slowly, backing away, more undulatingly, more desperately generous with her smiles than ever. No one was watching her, only Herman, out of the corner of his eye. They were mulling various strategies to get next summer's Parisians to consume more than ever before.

5 – Knowing that Charlotte's mother thought highly of him, Herman resolved to ask her a favor. He wanted, once—just once—to visit the shoe sellers' house, and he told her in all sincerity that he would

never know peace in the village until he could. It was an indelicate thing to do, possibly harmful to his own interests, and he knew it.

"But after that I'll never ask for anything again," he promised, "and whatever I can do to be helpful, I'll do it."

He simply had to see with his own eyes how Rose and the boy were lodged in their immortal village existence.

Charlotte's mother asked no questions. She went to see the shoe sellers, and they came to an agreement: On a certain afternoon of a certain day Herman would have a half hour to explore the house as he pleased. In gratitude, Herman bought the most expensive pair of rubber boots in the shop, along with slippers and espadrilles, and simultaneously he abandoned his intention of haggling with Charlotte's mother when she handed him his bill at the end of the month.

When the day came he entered the shop and headed straight upstairs, as agreed. The owners had gone out so he could look around at his leisure. The house was silent, dark, exceedingly proper and drab. Many doors opening onto little low-ceilinged rooms cluttered with the usual rustic furniture. Numb, trembling with dread, Herman softly called to Rose and the child. To his irritation he saw that his pant cuffs were dripping onto the wood floors. Two flights up, at the end of a hallway, he found a sort of storage room, dusty, furnished with two old straw-seat chairs. The little oval window looked out the back of the house, toward the hills atomized by the mist and the rain.

"This must be the place," thought Herman, looking at the two chairs side by side before the window.

This room seemed different from the others, with a very particular sort of silence—fuller, thicker—you could almost see it, could almost touch it. Rose's perfume, the pleasing scent of fresh soap that always emanated from the child's body, Herman breathed deep and was crushed to find that he couldn't smell a trace of either one. Another wave of irrational terror ran through him. He wanted to run. But just then they walked in, hand in hand, and sat down in the chairs, never letting go of each other. They'd walked silently straight past Herman in their soaked summer clothes. Rose had smiled at him, very formally, just as she'd done the last time. And now they were looking out at the almost invisible hilltops, sitting very straight in their chairs, motionless, and at the television relay tower whose top sometimes poked through the immovable mass of black clouds.

"So this is what they look at every day," murmured Herman, his fear subsiding.

He timidly called out to them. But he didn't dare

try to touch them. He felt overwhelmed by a feeling of aloneness, along with a renewed conviction that Rose's choice to settle forever among these hills would never bring her or him anything like happiness.

"But still, yes, we'll be glad we exist," he told himself. "There will be that, though nothing more."

Then he stopped calling out, realizing they couldn't hear. Fat drops of water rolled off their hair and onto the floor. The boy looked thinner than he remembered, his neck stiff, still, and cold. They joylessly stared out at the hills, remote and indifferent, and with a twinge of anger Herman found himself thinking he'd often seen them visibly happier than this in Paris. He sighed and walked out. Just then the telephone rang, downstairs. Herman reflexively hurried to answer it. He recognized the principal's voice.

"I called your hotel, you weren't there, and they gave me this number, so…"

He must have been calling from the teachers' lounge, because Herman heard adult voices, laughter, rustling papers, locker doors slamming shut. Here in the shoe sellers' dark living room, amid the stout, sturdy furniture, the silence was heavy, thick with the village's wintertime peacefulness. Herman shivered. He found it hard to speak in the same tone as before.

"You've been replaced, Monsieur Herman," the principal was saying, "starting today, that's what I have to tell you. I believe we gave you as much time as we could, I think you'll agree, but it's clear your relocation is now complete. That said, Monsieur Herman, you have all our sympathy, and all our understanding."

Herman stammered, unable to come up with the words and the phrasing to be used with a superior. He found nothing in his mind but slightly over-colloquial expressions about the rain or the temperature, or "You said it," or "Well, gotta get going," which he used freely with Charlotte, but which were no good to him here. He decided to say nothing, punctuating the principal's explanations with only a few noncommittal mumbles. The restless, garrulous life he could hear going on through the phone had become alien to him, almost frightening. What could he possibly have to say, here in the numbing silence of the shoe sellers' living room?

"Well, good-bye," he said when he sensed the principal was finished.

"Good-bye, good-bye, Monsieur Herman, good-bye…"

Now no one had any reason to call him from Paris, he thought as he hung up. He was alone, all alone. The intangible forms upstairs didn't seem to care that he was here in the village. Deep inside, Herman was hurt that Rose hadn't chosen a house where she could gaze at him day and night, like Alfred's wife, that she'd opted for the view of the misty, rain-shrouded hills. It's true that she would then have seen him in bed with Charlotte or Métilde or perhaps someone else (if that ever came to pass), but still, Herman would have felt less profoundly alone.

6 – Eventually Herman could stall Gilbert no longer. When he came to see Herman one morning and announced that the tennis match with his friend Lemaître was scheduled for that day in L., there was nothing to do but hurry to get ready and climb into the passenger seat of Gilbert's car. Gilbert was keyed up, anxious and fidgety. He smelled strongly of cologne. Herman thought he'd even put on a touch of makeup: his pale eyes highlighted by a black line, like an actor's, his colorless lips discreetly pinker now. He drove out of the village at an excessive speed, then raced along the little road to L., thirty kilometers away, the pavement almost invisible in the murk. Herman couldn't see the fields or trees on either side of them. They sped through a tunnel of mist now and then pierced by the headlights of the few oncoming, strangely silent cars. Gilbert's fervor, his odd appearance, the slightly feminine scent he'd doused himself with, all that heightened Herman's unease, his

suspicion that he was running a risk by leaving the village.

"Still, I really do have to take out some money," he thought to convince himself this trip was necessary.

Alfred had loaned him a sweater and hunting jacket, but he felt as damp as ever. And once they'd passed by the village's last house, Herman thought himself a man condemned. He'd never been to L., which Gilbert and Métilde inevitably described as the very antithesis of the dreary, pathetic village. But Herman couldn't help but think that he too was a lost soul now, and lost souls never leave the place they choose or end up in. He tried to laugh all that off, to tell himself he was being stupid, but in his mounting anxiety he was starting to find it hard to breathe. Gilbert wasn't saying a word, so Herman asked him about his friend Lemaître—and just why was it so vital that Herman partner with Gilbert in this doubles match?

Gilbert let out a glum little laugh and protested that Lemaître wasn't his friend, that people like Lemaître—a district councilor and a swimming-pool builder—felt nothing but disdain for villagers like Gilbert, even though he was the son of a merchant. The fact was that when you came from the village you couldn't possibly hope a Lemaître might see you as an equal, however kind and affectionate he was with you.

Gilbert knew that to Lemaître (a native of L.) he was simply a hick, too backward even to pass the bacca-lauréat, but by some miracle endowed with physical attributes (handsomeness, presence, etc.) that made him worth spending time with, eclipsing his deplor-able origin just enough to let it be forgotten—even as he treated Gilbert with all the condescension and dismissiveness that went with the degrading nimbus of the village enveloping his agile young body. So no, you couldn't call Lemaître his friend. But Gilbert had worked his magic on him. The man was seduced, that was certain. And now Lemaître would have no choice but to help him. It was in Lemaître's power to get him into the First School of Commerce without a degree. It wasn't exactly kosher, but Lemaître had the means. Except he wasn't the type to bestow favors purely out of friendship.

"Ha, ha, that's for sure!" Gilbert laughed, his up-per lip now glistening with sweat.

Lemaître liked a little fun, he liked making bets. They'd agreed that if Gilbert won the match Lemaître would pull the necessary strings at the school for Gilbert and never ask anything more of him. If not, Gilbert would have to find some way to purchase his help. That was fair. Because what chance did Gilbert have of getting anywhere without a leg up from Lemaître? He would vegetate in the village, with nothing to do, drifting from internship to internship, at best he would wind up in some lowly, demoralizing little job like janitor at the cider works or asphalt layer, obscure city office worker or summer factotum for the Parisians. He wasn't going to let that happen, not for anything in the world. Whatever the price to satisfy Lemaître and get his support, Gilbert would pay it; he would never resign himself to letting go and languishing his life away in the village.

"Yes, well, I did tell you I haven't played tennis for twenty years," Herman fretted.

He shifted unhappily this way and that in his seat. He was angry at Gilbert for picking him as a partner when he hardly knew how to play, placing the responsibility for an almost certain defeat on his feeble, shivering shoulders.

"Oh, it doesn't matter that much," said Gilbert.

But he gunned the engine, sped up even more. His eyelids twitched nervously as he strained to make out the edges of the pavement. Already he had dark makeup smudges at the corners of his eyes. He rolled down his window and took a deep breath. Herman felt as if the water that had replaced the blood in his veins was beginning to freeze, and he knew for certain that nothing would ever warm him again.

"You know, the big thing," Gilbert explained, "is for him to see that I know someone from Paris, that

I'm not so…that I'm even friends with a Parisian, because apparently he knows a ton of them, but he doesn't play tennis with them or anything, whereas I…he'll have to admit I've got him beaten there…"

And that, he explained, would earn him a glory far more precious than he would ever get from possibly winning the match. Too bad if he then had to sacrifice himself to Lemaître. Besides, he will have brought Herman, so Lemaître would treat him a little more respectfully. Herman still had his magnificent Parisian face that would shut Lemaître up.

"You don't mind too much, I hope?" Gilbert asked softly.

But Herman couldn't bring himself to answer. He slumped against the car door and closed his eyes, so furious with himself for leaving the village that he was trembling all over in fear and resentment.

Gilbert parked his car on the main square of L. and walked Herman to the tennis club, where they would all sit down for lunch before the match. Destroyed in the last war, the subprefecture city of L. had been entirely rebuilt in concrete and brick. The town center consisted of three pedestrian streets lined with low apartment buildings, flat-roofed, their balconies fronted with tinted plastic. Herman was a little taken aback: was that really all there was to L.? The streets were almost deserted in the falling rain.

The cobblestones were slippery, the flower pots half filled with bottles and wax-paper wrappers.

"Oh, Métilde!" cried Herman, spotting a young woman walking ahead of them, hunched under an umbrella.

But she turned a corner, and the club lay straight ahead. Herman wanted to go after her.

"No time," said Gilbert.

"She would have saved me," thought Herman, suddenly resigned. Because he knew Métilde didn't have a car, and never went to L. It would be another six months before she hoped to be driven there for the exam. So why would she be here, if not, providentially, just for him? To take him back to the village, to help him go home? But she hadn't seen him, and in his great weakness around Gilbert he'd let her slip away.

And now they were at the tennis club, Gilbert on edge, forcing himself to whistle, slapping his thigh with his racket. He'd recognized Lemaître's massive 4x4 outside, and now he was peering around for him in the restaurant that overlooked the tennis courts, roofed for the season. Catching him off guard after the dull, empty streets, the tumult in the club filled Herman with anguish. He put his hands over his already aching ears, but the violent music pouring from a dozen speakers in the ceiling, the hubbub of voices in the packed room, and the balls being batted back and forth on the court below had exploded in his skull the moment he came in, and now his head was vibrating, resonating, ringing absurdly. He turned to flee, but Gilbert clasped his elbow and herded him toward Lemaître's table, just by the balustrade, with a view of the games going on below.

"The other one will be here after lunch," Gilbert whispered, meaning Lemaître's partner.

He gave Lemaître a quick embrace and made the introductions.

"Herman's from Paris," he launched in. "The fourteenth arrondissement, actually, right, Herman, the Rue des Plantes?"

"Say, I know someone who lives around there, a big deal," Lemaître shot back.

He was about Herman's age, but enormously taller and fatter. He was dressed in tight jeans, a floral tie, a striped shirt, his gray-white hair in a ponytail. He looked at Herman with an arrogant, incurious gaze. The whites of his eyes were generously veined with red. Herman felt him studying his narrow shoulders, his spindly arms, observing, perhaps with pleasure, the wetness in him and on him, his master inside and out.

"But in that case why are you still here with us, Monsieur Herman?"

"My wife wanted to stay," Herman murmured, and Lemaître seemed to understand.

Tortured by the noise, Herman couldn't repress a grimace. He was deeply ashamed to be there. He was betraying the village.

"We opened this club not six months ago, you won't find one like it even in Paris—there's squash, a sauna, a weight room, the works. Two million, it cost," Lemaître explained. "I brought the club to this city, yes, and it's changed things around here, believe me."

Without asking, Lemaître ordered the same meal for everyone. Then Gilbert set about talking up Herman, eager to make clear what an exceptional honor Herman had granted the village and its citizens by taking up residence there, because Herman was a pure Parisian, etc. He punctuated every sentence, recited in a clipped, impassioned voice, with bursts of "Right? Right?" aiming to bring Herman into the conversation. But although he would have liked to oblige Gilbert, Herman didn't speak, his jaw frozen, unable to open his mouth. He sat slumped in his chair, staring down at the table, paralyzed by dread: the village seemed so far away now... Who would take him back, who would see that he got there safe and sound? Lemaître gave him a sardonic look. Ever more tense and red-faced, Gilbert was now claiming that Herman got phone calls from Paris every day.

"Right?" he threw out in a sharp voice, his eyes ablaze.

He leaned over to shake Herman's shoulder. Herman nodded. Gilbert shot him a livid look all the same. Lemaître let out a condescending little snicker, then fleetingly caressed Gilbert's cheek and announced that he'd just sold a horseshoe-shaped swimming pool to so-and-so, the owner of an estate, he went on at great length about those people, they'd become great friends of his.

"Who will take me back, who will pardon me?" thought Herman to the tune of the song blaring from the loudspeakers.

Gilbert drew himself up and announced that he too would like to know people who swim in horseshoe-shaped pools. He was eager to make some connections, he declared. The region was loaded with rich, high-rolling, elegant people—the kind of people who have pieds-à-terre in Paris—if only he could be one of them, someday... Armed with a solid degree in business administration, freed from the grip of the village, he'd have no trouble fitting into that world, a world so perfectly suited to his tastes—and so close, it was all around the village and L., nestled deep in almost inaccessible valleys where unimaginable manor houses and châteaux could be glimpsed (a turret, a dovecote) from the highway.

"Yes, yes," Lemaître nodded, at once tickled and scornful.

Herman was wondering: "Will the village take me back? Will I ever see it again?"

Then, making a supreme effort, raising his head and squaring his shoulders, he pushed back his chair and barked:

"I'm all out of cash, I've got to go withdraw some money!"

He turned his back to Gilbert and Lemaître, uncertainly wended his way between the tables, and, once outside, jumped the three front steps to the sidewalk. He fell and scraped his hands.

"Oh, there you are," said Métilde, appearing before him.

She helped him up, visibly relieved to have found him at last, then kept her arm clasped around his waist for a few steps, her other hand gripping her big pink umbrella.

"We have to walk faster," she said. "We don't want them catching us."

Herman clung to the belt of Métilde's raincoat. Her fresh, pale, determined face, her brow slightly tinted by the light filtering through the umbrella, all of it filled him with thirst and temptation. She walked with a vigorous gait, pulling Herman along. Weak in the legs, he let himself be led.

"When I heard you'd left with Gilbert for the great tennis match," Métilde explained, "I went and stood by the road to hitch a ride. No, I've never done that before. I did it for you; I wanted to stop you from playing if there was still time, because you're in no condition for tennis, you'd pass out, it's not safe. Yes, I told Gilbert, again and again, but he refused to see the terrible things our climate is doing to you. Your body's worn down by the cold and the rain, it's only natural, you're not from around here, you're not ready for…"

Suddenly the rain was falling harder, the sky turning black, the wind picking up. The umbrella turned inside out. Métilde pushed Herman under the arcades. He didn't realize it, but he was still hunching, and stood a head shorter than her.

"So, the storms have come," said Métilde. "We're not going to get back today, no car would ever go out on the roads between here and the village. Come on, hurry, let's get a room at the inn."

Herman let out a little moan as she dragged him into the street and ordered him to run after her. The rain was falling so hard that it felt like someone was knocking on his head with a stick, his head that still ached from the din at the club. He struggled to follow Métilde as she bounded among the puddles that pocked the dreary pedestrian street, deploying all the strength of her muscular calves. And if he hadn't bent down and thrown himself forward, the wild wind would have knocked him flat on his face.

"This is horrible, it's horrible…"

He groaned softly to himself, convinced his final hour had come. Métilde laughed as they entered the inn.

"How we loved the storms when we were little," she said, gaily tossing her hair.

Exhausted, Herman was about to lean on her shoulder, but he froze when he glanced through the glass door to the sitting room and spotted Rose's parents, in matching armchairs, holding glasses of water and looking slightly uncomfortable. He jerked away from Métilde. He felt like he was about to drop to the floor, drained by surprise, despair, and exhaustion.

"What on earth is it?" asked Métilde.

"My in-laws."

"Where?"

"There, in the sitting room," Herman whispered, not looking at her.

Just then they caught sight of him. The father leaped to his feet, opened the door, and took Herman in his arms. Relieved and ashamed, Herman noticed that Métilde had turned away, giving no sign that she knew him, and was now asking the desk clerk for a single room. Next it was the mother's turn to embrace him, her eyes brimming with tears.

"It's so good to see you, my little Herman, it's so good."

She held on for a moment longer, her arms around his neck.

"But you don't look well at all!" the father cried. "You've melted, you've literally melted!"

"Don't go nagging him about his appearance," said the mother.

"But just look at him, it's like he's shrunk!"

"It's this place, this dreadful place," she answered, stepping back for a better look at Herman.

"Good God," the father exclaimed in dismay, "the cold, the rain, this sinister town. I've never seen anything like it. It's as dark as midnight! Where are Rose and the little one, dear Herman?"

"They stayed behind in the village."

Herman went into the sitting room and collapsed onto a couch. The parents were still wearing their coats, blowing into their hands, clapping for warmth. They seemed so displeased by what they were finding in L. that their almost virtuous indignation drowned out their disappointment, and they looked around them with outraged, unbelieving glances, full of upright reproof. Rose's parents lived in the southwest. They were both short, lively, and excitable; their skin was dusky, their speech quick and sharp. They weren't fond of traveling, which made Herman all the more surprised and befuddled to find them here in L. They sat down close to him, on the very edges of their seats, their feet impatiently tapping the floor, and the mother finally explained what they were doing there, her voice suddenly turning reproachful:

"You understand, we called to ask how the child was getting along in the new school year, we called morning and night, and all we ever got was the answering machine talking about a vacation, but the vacation was supposed to have been over, wasn't it, we knew the dates, so what were we supposed to think? We were getting worried, it was awful! So, well, one day, I said, 'All right, if they're still there, then let's go pay them a visit out at their vacation house, we can discover the region, it will be an adventure for us, and at the same time we'll find out why Herman and the boy aren't at school.' We took the train, eight hours, and here we are—we got in just this morning. But really now, you could have told us. I mean we're happy to be here, but still, that wasn't right of you, yes, Rose is going to hear from me. And then the storm came, we wanted to take a taxi to the village but they told us no one would travel on the roads today, we'd have to wait till tomorrow or the day after. Infuriating! We had to come to the inn, get a room; you can imagine how thrilled we were to be stuck here in L., but

evidently there's no other way. What a place, it's in-
credible, it's appalling…"

Now the mother seemed deeply frightened. She
squeezed her jacket collar shut with an anxious hand.

"Herman, you said the sky was always blue here."

"It is, until the thirty-first of August, but then…"

"How can people live… And this city, Herman,
it's just a lot of hideous apartment buildings, all
thrown up any old way."

"The war," said Herman.

"Oh yes, the war."

The father's demeanor turned grave and pious.
An infinite sadness descended over the dimly lit sitting room. The mother cocked her head and seemed
to be listening for the sound of the long-ago bombs.

"We never had to go through that back home,"
she said. "No, we never lacked for anything, did we?"

"We have no right to complain," answered the
father.

They fell silent, downcast. Herman was afraid the
conversation might come back to Rose and the child.
And what was he supposed to do with these two old
people tomorrow?

"And this weather, these gray skies, is that because of the war too?" the mother asked in a quaver-
ing voice, staring into the distance.

Just then Métilde walked past the glass door.

Herman didn't have the courage to stand up and go to her and calmly explain what was happening, but he sensed that by letting Métilde go away hurt and angry he was losing his one chance to get back to the village.

They sat for a long time, all three of them silent and gloomy, as if benumbed by the old, musty smell of the shabbily furnished sitting room, and Herman found himself thinking this was the whole reason the parents were there: to bear witness—with their brightly colored athletic shoes, the cool, dark skin of their faces—to the very singular desolation visited in the fall on this once ravaged patch of the provinces. But this is where Herman wanted to stay. Suddenly he couldn't bear the thought of being away from the village any longer. And, unable to decide if it would be better for the parents to see Rose and the child or not, he told himself he would do everything he could to take them, come what may, and then they could draw whatever conclusions they liked—what could Herman change about what had happened?

"Let's see if we can go," he said abruptly. "Yes, let's try right now."

"What about the storm?" said the mother, clutching her thin jacket.

"Well, what about it?" the father said irritably, already on his feet. "He's offering to take you to your daughter. Come on, he knows what he's doing, we're strangers here, we don't know anything, do we?"

At the front desk, Herman asked for a taxi. It was so cold he could hardly move his lips.

"No taxi driver's going to go out in this weather," said the woman.

"I'm begging you," Herman whispered.

He leaned as far over the counter as he could and brought his exhausted but resolute eyes very close to hers.

"Find one. I'm begging you."

Behind him, Rose's mother cried, "Yes, yes, let's get out of this city!" as if, thought Herman, the war was still raging in L.

They went back to wait in the sitting room, the father nervously patting his knees, the mother saying over and over that she wasn't going to spend a single night in L., her lips going blue from the cold.

"All right, your taxi's here," the desk clerk came to say.

In a murmur, she added: "It's the worst taxi in L."

Herman tried to pick up his in-laws' suitcase, but his frail arms wouldn't let him, and the father, disturbed, remarked:

"You're in sad shape, my boy."

But he himself nearly collapsed when he unwarily strode through the hotel's front door and the rain hit him square in the chest. They piled into the car as best they could.

"It'll cost extra today, understand?" asked the driver.

He turned to them, his face fat and purple, and they saw that he had no nose. Rose's mother let out a little cry. Then, embarrassed, she put her face to the window and pretended to study the street.

"Whatever you like," Herman said quietly.

Resigned, he realized the man was drunk. The taxi reeked of wine. Slowly they drove out of L., the car already rocking and lurching in the wind.

"How ugly, how horrible this city is," the mother whispered; on the brink of tears, Herman thought.

The driver had heard her, and he raised one index finger high. Now they were out on the dark highway, driving so slowly that Herman was sure his liquefaction would be complete long before they got to the village.

The driver half turned around toward them, showing his perfectly flat profile, feverish, and told them:

"Yes, but you didn't know L. the way it was back in my day, long ago, it was beautiful, take my word for it, I was born there, I grew up there, before the war, it was a different place then, you should have seen it, old timber-framed houses, half-timbers, all leaning and crooked, then the war, the bombs, the fires, and then in the middle of all that off goes my nose, it was shrapnel, a chunk of my cheek blown away, and my whole nose along with it, 'Have you seen your nose? Where did your nose go?' I've been hearing that for the past fifty years, in every café in L., 'So-and-so has your nose in his pocket, my house is built on your nose,' that's perfectly possible, the rubble, it was in there, buried somewhere, my nose is somewhere in the ground under L., in its walls, I think about that all the time, you understand, I talk to it, I call out to it, I see it, it's poking out between two bricks, or when I'm walking downtown there it is stuck between two paving stones, that's my nose, and that, right, how can you ever forgive that, how can you forgive..."

As he spoke, he slapped his face just above his mouth over and over again.

"Ha ha!" snickered Rose's father.

He looked at Herman and made a gesture like he was twisting his nose, to signify that the driver was drunk.

"Ha ha," murmured Herman.

Then the car slowed to a stop; the driver cursed, pounded the wheel.

"There we go, she's died on us!" he cried.

MARIE NDIAYE was born in 1976 in Pithiviers, France. She is the author of around twenty novels, plays, collections of stories, and nonfiction books, which have been translated into numerous languages. She's received the Prix Femina and the Prix Goncourt, France's highest literary honor, and her plays are in the repertoire of the Comédie-Française.

JORDAN STUMP is one of the leading translators of innovative French literature. The recipient of numerous honors and prizes, he has translated books by Nobel laureate Claude Simon, Jean-Philippe Toussaint, and Éric Chevillard, as well as Jules Verne's French-language novel *The Mysterious Island*. His translation of NDiaye's *All My Friends* was shortlisted for the French-American Foundation Translation Prize.